"Tell me, Sarah, who taught you to say *I can't* so eloquently?" Brad murmured. Intentness replaced the teasing expression in his green eyes.

"I don't know what you mean," she countered.

"You *shouldn't* go for a walk with me, you *aren't* good at guessing, you *can't* dance in the streets just because the spirit moves you—whoever told you there were so many things you *shouldn't* and *couldn't*?"

Sarah drew herself up with a deep breath and met his searching gaze head on. "I'm twenty-eight years old, your honor, and I decide for myself what I will and will not do. Did it ever occur to you that my responses might have been a subtle, polite way of saying I just don't want to?"

He smiled down at her, apparently unperturbed by the storm warning in her eyes. "I did consider that possibility briefly. I dismissed it for one blatantly obvious reason: You're enjoying this every bit as much as I am." He pulled her tightly against him without breaking eye contact. "And I *am* enjoying it, Sarah. Much more than I was prepared to..."

Dear Reader:

We're celebrating SECOND CHANCE AT LOVE's third birthday with a new cover format! I'm sure you had no trouble recognizing our traditional butterfly logo and distinctive SECOND CHANCE AT LOVE type. But you probably also noticed that the cover artwork is considerably larger than before. We're thrilled with the new look, and we hope you are, too!

In a sense, our new cover treatment reflects what's been happening *inside* SECOND CHANCE AT LOVE books. We're constantly striving to bring you fresh and original romances with unexpected twists and delightful surprises. We introduce promising new writers on a regular basis. And we aim for variety by publishing some romances that are funny, some that are poignant, some that are "traditional," and some that take an entirely new approach. SECOND CHANCE AT LOVE is constantly evolving to meet your need for "something new" in your romance reading.

At the same time, we *haven't* changed the successful editorial concept behind each SECOND CHANCE AT LOVE romance. And we've consistently maintained a reputation for being a line of the highest quality.

So, just like the new covers, SECOND CHANCE AT LOVE romances are satisfyingly familiar—yet excitingly different—and better than ever!

Happy reading,

Ellen Edwards

Ellen Edwards, Senior Editor
SECOND CHANCE AT LOVE
The Berkley Publishing Group
200 Madison Avenue
New York, N.Y. 10016

P.S.   Do you receive our SECOND CHANCE AT LOVE and TO HAVE AND TO HOLD newsletter? If not, be sure to fill out the coupon in the back of this book, and we'll send you the newsletter free of charge four times a year.

Second Chance at Love®

TOUCH OF MOONLIGHT

LIZ GRADY

A SECOND CHANCE AT LOVE BOOK

Other Second Chance at Love books by
Liz Grady

TOUCH OF MOONLIGHT

First edition published August 1984

First printing

"Second Chance at Love," and the butterfly emblem are trademarks belonging to Jove Publications, Inc.

Printed in the United States of America

Second Chance at Love books are published by
The Berkley Publishing Group
200 Madison Avenue, New York, NY 10016

To Mom and Dad

For their love and encouragement
and for giving me a start
in the right direction

Chapter One

SARAH TEMPLETON PACED restlessly to the window and edged the white lace curtain aside for a discreet peek at the narrow street below. It was still as empty as the last time she'd checked . . . and the time before that.

Not that she even knew what she was checking for. The last time she'd been out on a blind date, it had been with a sixteen-year-old driving the family station wagon. She was fairly certain that Brad Chandler, a Rhode Island Superior Court judge and the man her friend Julie insisted was the answer to all Sarah's prayers, would be driving something more befitting his suave, sophisticated image.

His *reputedly* suave and sophisticated image, she qualified, letting the curtain slip back into place. She didn't see anything suave or sophisticated about arriving late, even if this was only a blind date, and even if it was only by three and a half minutes.

Impatiently she strode across the living room, stopping at the oval mirror to recheck her lipstick, run a comb through the already perfect layers of her dark,

1

shoulder-length hair, and anguish all over again about whether the deep blue silk dress with its narrow straps and ruffled bodice was really the right choice after all. It wasn't what she would ordinarily choose for a business dinner, but then, this wasn't exactly a business dinner. At least, Brad Chandler wasn't supposed to know it was.

That gave her a whole new subject to anguish over: what sort of ludicrous tale Julie had spun to talk him into agreeing to this date with Sarah in the first place. Not the truth, of that Sarah was certain. Julie had warned her that if Brad even suspected the real reason for tonight's meeting, he would bolt in the opposite direction. Besides, the truth was seldom colorful or bizarre enough to suit Julie. Thoughts of what her friend might have substituted for it turned Sarah's already damp palms downright clammy, making her wonder, not for the first time, why she was going along with this.

The answer came to her along with a small, rueful smile. She had no choice. Miriam Blakely, the publisher of *Inside Newport,* had come up with the brilliantly tasteless idea of doing an article on the ten sexiest men in Newport, and, after exhausting every logical argument, Sarah, as editor, had gracefully acquiesced. Now she had five days to come up with several viable candidates and, as her old pal Julie had so obligingly pointed out, absolutely no idea where to start looking.

The sudden chiming of the doorbell signaled that her search was about to begin. Reminding herself that this evening was really business, even if Mr. Chandler didn't know it, she crossed slowly to the front door, pausing en route to stuff the overflow of magazines back into the wicker rack and nudge a tennis shoe, which had suddenly appeared from nowhere, under the nearest chair. As she gripped the knob and swung the oak door open wide, it occurred to Sarah that she was uniquely unqualified to spend a carefree evening with one of the ten sexiest men anywhere. The thought brought on a rush of belated panic not unlike what she'd felt all those years ago climbing into that beat-up station wagon.

One glance at Brad Chandler warned Sarah that he was a far cry from her last blind date, and that if appearances counted for anything, Julie's assessment had been right on the money. He was tall and lean, with the promise of hard muscularity beneath the perfectly fitting gray suit and soft white shirt. Dark chestnut hair, thick and full, was combed carelessly back from a face that stopped short enough of being handsome to give the chiseled cheekbones, straight nose, and distractingly sensual mouth an intriguing quality. The overall effect was one of strength and determination, tempered only by the dimples in his cheeks. And those dimples were deepening in direct proportion to the wattage of his faintly curious smile.

"Sarah?" he inquired tentatively in a deep, velvety baritone, sweeping her with a look that sent an inexplicable shiver rippling along her spine.

Sarah stared into his smoky green eyes, wondering at the vague look of puzzlement that was causing tiny fans of lines to form at their outer corners, until she realized she still hadn't answered.

"Yes, I'm Sarah," she said hurriedly. "You must be Brad."

"Right." He heaved a sigh of relief that she suspected wasn't totally feigned. "Am I glad that's out of the way! At the risk of being considered hopelessly old-fashioned, I brought these for you."

"Lilies of the valley!" she exclaimed, accepting the bouquet of tiny white buds and bringing it to her nose to sniff their delicate fragrance. "My favorite flower."

"Then I'm glad I stopped, even if it did mean getting here a few minutes late."

It wasn't an apology exactly, but then, Brad Chandler didn't exactly look like the apologetic type. Sarah hadn't decided yet what type he was, except to note with instinctive certainty that it wasn't hers. She would never admit it, but Julie had been right about another thing. In recent years Sarah's choice of males seemed to run to the skinny, bespectacled, and sexually unthreatening. The man standing on her doorstep was a dismal failure on all three counts.

"I don't know..." he began hesitantly as the silence between them lengthened awkwardly. "Do they look a little thirsty to you?" His head was tilted to the side in a gesture of concern, but the expression in the piercing green eyes was one of pure devilment.

For a second, Sarah continued to stare; then her gaze dropped to the flowers in her hand and she took a step backward. "Of course. Come on in while I put them in some water. I know I have a vase here somewhere."

She knew nothing of the kind, but it seemed reasonable that somewhere in the gloomy depths of the kitchen cupboards she was forever vowing to clean out there would be something that could pass for a vase. After long moments of frantic searching, during which she was acutely aware of Brad watching her from the doorway, she settled for an old jelly glass and hoped he wouldn't notice. He did.

"Smiling Strawberry," he announced, lifting the glass of flowers from the out-of-the-way table where she'd deposited them. "I like Goofy Grape myself, almost as much as I like women who use jelly glasses instead of crystal vases. It's very homey." He glanced around the room furnished with a congenial blend of old and new. "Just like your apartment."

His smile was warm, approving, stealing the breath from Sarah's lungs and sending all the clever one-liners she'd rehearsed spinning out of mind's reach.

"I meant that as a compliment," he added in the face of her silence.

"I'm sorry," she replied, fumbling for a passable excuse for her suddenly wandering wits. "I guess my mind is still back at the office. We're planning several big features for the summer issues, and I'm swamped with work."

"Then you're in luck. I happen to be a very good listener, and you have the whole evening to use me as a sounding board for your ideas."

She smiled back at him, until it hit her like a ton of bricks that *she* was the one who was supposed to be doing the listening tonight. "Oh, no. I could never bore you with all that. Besides, I'd much rather hear about your work."

He winced and reached for the embroidered shawl that lay on the arm of the sofa. "Now you're talking about heavy boredom, but we can fight it out once we're in the car. I made dinner reservations for eight o'clock at the Black Pearl, and traffic is already tied up around the wharf."

Luckily, Brad turned out to be a good talker as well. Between that and Sarah's renewed resolve to keep her mind on her mission, she managed to learn quite a bit about the everyday life of a Superior Court justice during the short drive to Bannister's Wharf. Far from being bored, she found herself mesmerized by the sometimes sad, sometimes hilarious tales of his experiences on the bench. She was almost disappointed when he broke off and pulled into a parking lot a few blocks from the wharf.

"I think the fastest way to get there is to walk the rest of the way, if that's all right with you."

Sarah smiled. "That sounds fine. It'll help me work up an appetite."

The streets surrounding Newport's waterfront tourist district were narrow and teeming with people in cars and on foot.

"It looks as if Cup fever has already taken hold," she observed, nodding toward a particularly rowdy group of tourists. Their Topsiders and jaunty nautical sportswear marked them as among the hordes of sailing enthusiasts

who'd already started arriving in town for the America's
Cup preliminary trials, which were still nearly a month
away.

Brad laughed as one rather unsteady member of the
troop wobbled into the middle of the street to play cross-
ing guard for the cheering crowd. "Just think," he said,
placing a hand under her elbow as they stepped off the
curb, "things will get a lot crazier before it's over. By
the time the actual race starts in September, you won't
even be able to *move* around here."

Glancing up at him, Sarah saw that he looked as
delighted as he sounded at the prospect. "Why, Brad
Chandler, you're a Cup groupie!"

"Yeah, but you have to promise not to tell anybody.
I have my image to preserve."

Sarah dropped her head to hide the guilty flush suddenly heating her cheeks. She wasn't planning to tell a
soul...except for the thousands of people who read
Inside Newport every month. Her silent attempt to ratio-
nalize her deception by telling herself she was simply
scouting potential candidates was interrupted by Brad.

"I don't think the citizens of Rhode Island would be
pleased to learn that the real reason I call all those lengthy
recesses is so I can catch the latest Cup results on the
TV in my chambers."

"You don't!" A hint of suspicion infiltrated Sarah's
amusement. "Do you?"

Smirking very smugly, he gave a casual shrug. "Do
you really think I'd ever confirm something like that to
a reporter?"

"I'm not a reporter," she declared, uneasiness adding
a touch of heat to her denial. "I'm the editor of *Inside
Newport.*"

"Same difference to a publicity-shy public servant."

His quick wink announced that he was only teasing,
but it was hitting far too close to home for Sarah to glibly
play along. "It's not the same thing at all. An editor has

nothing to do with researching or writing a story, at least not technically."

"Whoa, hold on." He used his hold on her elbow to draw her to a halt. "I was only joking. I certainly didn't mean to make light of your position."

The sincere apology reflected in his eyes only compounded her guilt. "You didn't. I just overreacted."

"It must be this foolish blind date business. It always brings out the worst in people." He smiled and gave her arm a gentle squeeze. "What do you say that, here and now, we officially declare this a non-blind date?"

Sarah smiled back at him, finding it an increasingly easy thing to do. "Then how shall we say we wound up together?"

"We could always pretend I picked you up on the corner."

She pretended to ponder for a moment, then shook her head firmly. "Uh-uh. That doesn't do any more for my self-image than a blind date does."

"I've got it. Why don't we just pretend we're two people who like each other, out enjoying an evening together?"

Her breath lodged in her throat under his softly attentive gaze. A small nod of agreement was all she could manage as the glittering green gaze navigated a slow path to her lips, then lower, in a languorous perusal that left her tinglingly aware of his approval.

When his eyes found their way back to hers, he said softly, "Good. Now that we've got that settled, I'm starving."

The Black Pearl was only a few steps away. It seemed natural for Brad's hand to slide down from her elbow to grasp hers firmly. What didn't seem natural to Sarah was the lightning that ricocheted through her veins at his touch. In bolts of varying intensity it lingered while they dined at a small, candlelit table overlooking the harbor.

Rather than having to subtly fish for information as

she'd expected, she discovered their conversation flowed effortlessly. They touched on a variety of topics—his talents as a chef, the respective agonies of being an only child, as he was, as opposed to the fourth of four, as she was—and it wasn't until the last bite of crêpes Chantilly had disappeared that she realized that somewhere along the way she'd forgotten her role of interrogator and had begun enjoying the evening.

Enjoying it much too much, she chided herself. After all, despite Brad's playful declaration to the contrary, this was still a blind date. One he had no doubt been coerced into by Julie, and one that would come to a very final end when he returned her to her door in a short while. Without a doubt, Brad's reputation as a charmer was richly deserved, but Sarah knew well the bottom line. Men like Brad weren't interested in women like her. Not for long, anyway. It was much safer emotionally to keep in mind that tonight was strictly business, and emotional safety was a way of life for Sarah Templeton.

Stepping out of the restaurant, Brad caught her hand in his and started strolling away from the spot where they'd left the car. "Let's walk for a while. It's a beautiful night."

"No, really, I shouldn't." The words, promoted by years of zealous caution, tumbled out unbidden. But not unwisely, Sarah told herself. She was torn between the knowledge that she'd accomplished her objective and should now bring the evening to a quick close and the reckless desire to keep walking, hand in hand with Brad, through the warm, star-touched night.

His gently quizzical eyes captured hers. "Why not?"

The question was so direct, so simple; the answer was layered with doubts and insecurities Sarah preferred not to explore. "It's getting late."

Eyebrows raised, he checked his watch. "Ten-thirty? I had no idea I was out with Cinderella." Without waiting for the flustered reply she was having difficulty making, he tucked her arm securely under his and continued walking. "Come on, Sarah. Let's play ship's names."

"Ship's names?" she echoed, having no choice but to tag along as he stepped onto a wooden dock that stretched thirty yards into the night-darkened harbor.

"Right. Whenever I walk along the docks like this I try to see how many of the ship's names I can guess." He stopped next to a long, sleek cabin cruiser bobbing in the light surf and peered into the dimly lit interior. "Like this one. Get a load of those preppy stripes. And those green-and-navy seat cushions. This has to be named something like *Muffy's Own*."

Sarah leaned over to read the block letters on the side. *"Windrider."*

"I was close." His broad shoulders lifted in a nonchalant shrug. "You try the next one."

"I can't. I wouldn't know what to guess."

"Just take a good look at her," he prompted, pressing Sarah's arm closer to his side, making her nerves shimmer with awareness of him, "and say the first thing that comes into your mind."

"Lucky Lady." Afraid even darkness wouldn't hide the flush that followed her impetuous words, she turned back toward the ship with a nervous laugh. "How did I do?"

"About the same as me. This one's called *Bitter Victory*. Probably part of a divorce settlement."

Their laughter mingled in the velvet night. "This is crazy," asserted Sarah. "Have you ever gotten one right?"

"No," he admitted, "but that doesn't mean I never will."

Urging Sarah to join in, he called out one wrong name after another as they strolled to the end of the dock, making her laugh almost to the point of tears with his inane attempts.

"No more," she pleaded as they reached the safety barrier. "I can't take any more."

"One more." His voice was suddenly rough velvet. "And I know I'm going to get this right. This one has to be *My Beautiful, Blue-eyed Lady*."

He wasn't even looking at the ship beside them. His eyes on hers were alight with something that alarmed Sarah and made her senses whirl at the same time. He turned her to face him fully, his hands light on her waist, his leaning position against the barrier bringing their faces breathtakingly close.

"I—I don't think there's even any blue on that boat," she stammered, amazed that words could still flow past the lump in her throat.

A slow smile teased the corners of his mouth. "Who's talking about boats?"

Chapter Two

"ALTHOUGH YOU MAY be right about the word *blue*," he continued, just as if the world hadn't stopped spinning on its axis, as if the heat generated by his closeness and the scorching look in his eyes hadn't short-circuited every sensory receptor in Sarah's body. "It's much too nondescript. It doesn't come close to capturing the real color of your eyes, the way they look like a summer sky in some lights and almost green in others, the way they sparkle when you smile. No one syllable could do justice to those eyes."

He lifted his hands and, with a touch as gentle as his tone, moved his fingers along the side of her face. "Or to the softness of your skin, or to the beautiful temptation of your mouth."

His thumb stroked downward as he spoke, lightly tracing the outline of her lips, making her breath freeze in her lungs. She was paralyzed under his touch, caught off guard by his unexpected familiarity, unable to move even if she'd wanted to, which she wasn't at all sure she did. Brad seemed to sense her stiffening, and an easy

11

smile drifted across his features as his hands moved down to catch both of hers. Bringing them to his lips, he placed a kiss in each palm, then curled her fingers over it.

"You're a challenge, Sarah Templeton. I may have to make up a whole dictionary of new words just to tell you how beautiful you are to me."

Of course, it was just a line. And probably a well-practiced one Sarah reminded herself as they strolled back toward the shore. Nonetheless, uttered in his deep, mesmerizing baritone, it held a potent magic, and she was still spellbound when he led her toward the courtyard at the center of the streets lined with boutiques and restaurants.

"I love all this," Brad said as they entered the court-yard overflowing with weekend revelers. "I know that by September we'll all be sick of stepping over street-corner jugglers and tired of listening to vendors hawking America's Cup T-shirts, but right now it's still fresh and new. It's as if the whole town is gearing up for something. Does that sound crazy?"

Sarah affected her most sophisticated air. "Not at all. Just because you like to mingle with the tourists and watch con artists selling invisible dogs on leashes to people who are old enough to know better is no reason anyone should consider you crazy. Or hokey," she added, biting the inside of her lip to hold the pose.

Brad grinned broadly and gave her hand a retaliatory squeeze. "Oh, yeah? Well, hokey or not, I like all this excitement. It makes me feel"—his head turned in the direction of the music spilling from the open door of a small club—"like dancing. Come on. Dance with me, Sarah."

"Not here! We can't," she replied automatically even as he pulled her toward a clear spot just outside the club. Then she was in his arms, his hold loose enough to be proper and close enough to start her moving with him to the slow beat of the music.

Dancing in the streets was just one of a long list of things Sarah never did, and it took several nervous moments before she relaxed sufficiently to realize that no one was giving them a second glance. That concern banished, she was free to concentrate on the way their bodies fit together, like interlocking pieces of a puzzle. Her high-heeled sandals made her the perfect height to nestle her head into the crook of his shoulder if she'd had a mind to. It felt good, so good, just being held in his arms. She angled her head up a bit, savoring the clean, citrus scent of aftershave that clung to his skin and noting the way his hair brushed the collar of his jacket, begging to be touched. So engrossed was she in absorbing every detail of the heavenly moment that her fingers, which had been knotted into a fist on his shoulder, uncurled to cling gently instead.

His breath was a warm mist in her ear as he murmured approvingly, "That's much better. This isn't so hard, is it?"

She tipped her head back, meeting his teasing grin with a small smile. "I suppose not."

"Tell me, Sarah, who taught you to say *I can't* so eloquently?"

A new intentness replaced the teasing expression in his green eyes, and Sarah instinctively lowered hers to study the subtle pattern of his silk tie. "I don't know what you mean," she countered, aiming for a lightness that fell flat.

"You *shouldn't* go for a walk with me, you *aren't* good at guessing, you *can't* dance in public just because the spirit moves you—whoever told you there were so many things you *shouldn't* and *couldn't*?"

Whether the charges he ticked off so casually were true or not, he had no right to grill her about it. Calling on an inner reservoir of determination she used every day in her job, Sarah drew herself up with a deep breath and met his searching gaze head on.

"I'm twenty-eight years old, your honor, and I decide for myself what I will and will not do. Did it ever occur to you that my responses might have been a subtle, polite way of saying I just don't want to?"

He smiled down at her, apparently unperturbed by the storm warning in her eyes. "I did consider that possibility briefly. I dismissed it for one blatantly obvious reason: You're enjoying this every bit as much as I am." He executed a very smooth turn and in the process pulled her tightly against him, all without breaking eye contact. "And I *am* enjoying it, Sarah. Much more than I was prepared to."

Sarah noted the enigmatic nature of his remark, but she was too busy getting a grip on the sensations his touch sent blazing through her to really consider it. His arm behind her had turned to velvet-covered steel, and their legs were molded together, severely limiting the pattern of their dance steps and rendering the simple act of breathing a task requiring her conscious effort.

Sarah chided herself for reacting to Brad like an affection-starved female, certain he could feel her heart pounding against his chest and guess the reason for it. She was equally certain he would release her instantly if she indicated such was her wish, and only one thing kept her from breaking away. He was right; she *was* enjoying it. Before she had a chance to come to her senses, the music ended.

With a graciousness she silently thanked him for, Brad let her go and easily guided them through the potentially awkward moments that followed. He continued to hold her hand as they ambled past shop windows, insisting they detour by the Sailmaker so he could show her the colors of the new sails he was having made. His boyish enthusiasm and his eagerness for her approval of his choice appealed to her on a level Sarah knew was unsafe.

"Uh-huh." She nodded, smiling. "Just as I suspected. Preppy green."

"That is *not* preppy green," he retorted, his tone and expression indignant. "There's actually very little green in it. It's turquoise. Almost the color of your eyes, I'd say." His own eyes warmed considerably as they locked with hers. "It's got to be an omen."

Sarah swallowed hard, unable to look away. "You must really love it."

"I think I'm beginning to." The soft acknowledgment was riddled with intimacy.

"I meant sailing," she corrected, aware of the silly grin plastered on her face yet unable to do anything about it.

"Oh, that." He chuckled with a trace of self-consciousness she hadn't expected him to possess. "How'd you guess?"

"Your tan," she answered truthfully, watching his dark eyebrows knit in confusion. "In New England at this time of year a tan like yours is a dead giveaway that you're a sailing fanatic."

"I think it's more like a permanent case of windburn," he explained as they resumed walking. "It probably adds another ten years' worth of wrinkles to the ones I've earned honestly in thirty-five years. But you're right; I do love it. Although, for me, the actual sailing is just part of the thrill. The real excitement comes from creating a boat that's a work of art."

"You build your own boats?"

"Parts of them," he answered with unmistakable pride. "I design them myself. Time and practicality dictate that some of the work be contracted out, but as much as possible they're mine from start to finish."

Sarah could hear his excitement in his animated tone, could feel it in the hand gripping hers. It infused her with a hundred questions she wanted to ask, none of them even remotely prompted by professional curiosity. "But how did you learn? Where do you do the actual work on them?"

He laughed, his eyes shining with pleasure at her interest. "I'm still learning, and I have a workshop out in back of my house. Once a design is perfected, I begin the framework construction there, then the hull is—" He broke off at her look of bewilderment. "How much do you know about boats?"

"Only that they float."

Their shared laughter was warm, comfortable. As they walked along, he carefully aimed his explanation of the sailboat-building process to her level of understanding, and they slipped into an easy companionship that went beyond the few hours they'd known each other. By the time he'd helped her into the black BMW and slipped behind the wheel, she was totally relaxed.

And totally unprepared for him to turn to her and say, "Come home with me, Sarah."

The surprised confusion she felt must have been mirrored on her face, for he laughingly added, "Not to see my etchings—I don't even have any. But I would like to show you what I'm working on. It's so seldom the women I date show any interest in it."

Years of practice sent the words "Thanks, maybe some other time" rolling to her tongue, but something made her bite them back. After all, seeing Brad's home and workshop *would* be a major help in drawing up a profile on him. Thrusting aside the inkling that it was Sarah-the-woman, not Sarah-the-editor, who wanted nothing more than to go home with him, she licked her lips and nodded. "Well, I'm very interested. I'd love to see your current project, Brad."

They kept up a steady patter as they drove along Ten Mile Ocean Drive, the winding two-lane route that curled along the coastline past some of the most spectacular homes in Newport. Before Sarah had exhausted her supply of seemingly casual questions, Brad tapped a button on the car's elaborate dashboard, and the towering wrought-iron gates of the estate on their left swung open for the BMW to pull through. Thousands of stars lit the spring night, making it easy for Sarah to see how the private drive curled around an ornate marble fountain. Beyond sprawled a house of burnished-gold brick, flanked by a velvety carpet of dark-green lawn and hedge-bordered formal gardens.

Brad smiled at her wide-eyed, openmouthed stare. "Now that I've succeeded in overwhelming you, I should point out that I don't actually live there." He pointed at the magnificent structure before them. "I live here."

They had veered off the central driveway and coasted to a halt beside a small bungalow set well away from the main house on the side nearest the ocean. Dogwood trees in full pink and white bloom formed a canopy above the car.

"The gatekeeper's house?" Sarah teased as she stepped from the BMW.

"It's called the guest house, but the truth is I felt more like a guest living alone in that other monstrosity after my folks retired to Florida. When I found myself begging the cook to eat dinner with me, just so I wouldn't have to face those other eleven empty chairs at the table, I knew it was time to move."

He took her first to his spacious workshop, where with unbounded enthusiasm he regaled her with the fine points of the work in progress on his drawing board. Surveying the design and listening to his detailed description of the new keel he was developing, Sarah couldn't suppress a smile of gentle amusement.

He broke off with an apologetic shrug. "You see what a little encouragement does to me? I'm probably boring you to tears."

"Not at all. But I have a hunch you might be in the wrong business. Does judge Chandler get half as excited over his work as sailor Chandler does?"

He stared at her for so long and with such a strange expression that Sarah wondered if her lighthearted remark had been misconstrued.

"Not by a long shot," he admitted finally, smiling with a blend of wonder and affection that she found thrilling, if a bit confusing. "Let's go on up to the house. I have a bottle of excellent brandy, and I promise not to say another word about sailing for the rest of the night."

The interior of Brad's home was a palette of warm earth tones, obviously designed to be comfortable and relaxing. Unfortunately, its distinctly masculine aura left Sarah feeling neither. While he poured the brandy she paced restlessly, willing herself to make a mental record of each detail. After all, that was her reason for being here, wasn't it? She eyed the rich redwood paneling and handwoven rugs, felt the nubby fabric of muted stripes covering the furniture. In the far corner of the living room stood a spiral staircase, and her gaze followed its curling path to the loft overhead, stopping abruptly when it reached the bed. It seemed mammoth, a shiny brass reminder of all the reasons it was dangerous to be here. Instantly the jitteriness she'd been holding at bay engulfed her.

She swung around just in time to plow into Brad, who was returning with two snifters of brandy. "Oh, I'm sorry," she exclaimed, taking an awkward step backward and stumbling on the leg of a chair in a scene straight out of a bad comedy.

"No damage done." He lowered the glasses to the tile-topped table near the sofa and reached for her hand. "Come over here, sit down, and relax."

His subtle emphasis on the word *relax* dashed any hope that she was presenting an air of cool sophistication, and Sarah thanked her lucky stars she at least managed to sink into the sofa with a modicum of grace. Long legs sprawled in front of him, Brad settled himself a discreet distance away. Still, she was overwhelmingly aware that he'd shed his tie and unbuttoned the top of his shirt, revealing a hint of softly curling dark hair beneath. As he leaned closer to hand her a glass of brandy, some scatterbrained instinct she hadn't even known she possessed overrode her uneasiness, making her wonder how far down his chest that thick mat went and if it could possibly feel as soft as it looked.

"To new friends," he said, raising his snifter. "Especially those who turn out to be such pleasant surprises."

His voice was pitched low, giving the toast a seductive shading that spurred a rising tide of apprehension in Sarah. She lifted the glass to her lips with one thought in mind: coming up with an excuse to get out of there. Quickly.

Stretching his arm along the back of the sofa, he angled himself to face her. "I just realized we've spent nearly the entire evening talking about me. You'll have to forgive me; I'm not usually so self-indulgent. You're just so easy to talk to, you make me feel . . . at ease. You're a very thoughtful woman."

"Not really." She shrugged uncomfortably, thrusting aside the thought of how "at ease" he would feel when he discovered the underlying reason for her avid interest in his activities. "I enjoyed hearing about your work and your hobbies. I'll bet lots of people would find you fascinating."

"Well, right this minute, I'm not interested in lots of people. I'm interested in you. I want to hear all about those magazine features you mentioned earlier."

The comment caught Sarah with her mouth full of brandy. She swallowed hard and promptly choked as the liquor burned a fiery trail down her throat.

"Are you all right?" Brad slid across the sofa cushion to pound her none too gently on the back. The force of it jarred the hand still holding the snifter, sending the brandy sloshing over the rim onto the sofa.

"Oh, I'm sorry! Look at this mess." She leaned forward, shoving the glass onto the table and managing to spill most of the rest of her drink in the process. "Oh, no. Your table."

"Forget the table," he growled. "I'm more concerned about you."

She waved her hand in a stab at casual detachment and croaked, "I'm fine."

"You don't sound fine." Frowning, he cupped her chin in his palm and tipped her face up. "You even have tears in your eyes."

"Yes, well, asphyxiation always makes me cry. Really, I'm fine now."

"And your fingers are like ice," he continued, ignoring her assurances and taking her hands firmly in his. "If it were winter I could warm you by the fire, but under the circumstances you'll have to settle for a more primitive technique."

The fervor in his gaze as he drew her slowly toward him left little doubt about the nature of the technique he intended to employ. Her well-honed instinct for self-preservation would have forced her to protest if that unfamiliar streak of flightiness hadn't suddenly reared its mutinous head, rendering her mesmerized by the smoky green depths of his eyes.

Brushing wispy waves of her sable hair back from her cheeks, he brought his lips to her ear, teasing it with a nibbling kiss. With slow, circular strokes he rubbed her ramrod-straight back and whispered, "You don't have to be afraid, Sarah. I only want to warm you, not devour you." Angling back, he slanted her a wicked grin. "At least not yet, anyway."

Before she could heed that veiled warning, he tilted his head and moved closer. His mouth, soft and supple, touched hers with infinite care, as if she were made of fine china. He moved with feather lightness at first, gradually increasing the pressure, parting his lips slightly and using the barest tip of his tongue to make hers slick. With each gentle stroke Sarah felt herself relaxing, falling further under the potent spell of his touch.

Vaguely she was aware of him easing her back on the cushion, sensed his fingers moving through her hair and drifting over her bare shoulders. New life permeated every cell of her body as his caress and kiss became more aggressive, urging her participation. He tasted and coaxed with a practiced expertise that went far beyond her power to resist. Physical cravings that had long lain dormant surged to bloom as his chest pressed closer, but her emotions were a churning mixture of excitement and anxiety. Just as excitement was gaining the edge, Brad eased away with a deep groan, and some semblance of reason returned to her.

"Brad," she started, attempting to straighten up, only to have his warm hands close over her shoulders and hold her firmly in place. "I don't think—"

"That's right," he interrupted with a lazy smile. "Don't think, Sarah."

Again his lips closed over hers, and this time the hesitancy and the tentativeness that had marked their first kiss was gone. Still gentle, he nonetheless moved against her more intently, demanding what he had earlier coaxed. True to his promise, he was warming her, scorching her with his touch. Beyond conscious thought, she was swept up in his ardor, and her lips parted to accept the rough heat of his tongue. His exploration of the recesses of her mouth was deep and thorough, eliciting a response Sarah hadn't known was hers to give. From somewhere far away she heard a small whimper and realized it was hers.

The realization filled her nicely warmed body with a sudden chill. Her hands, which had been weaving their way through the chestnut hair curling against his collar, jerked downward to push against the solid wall of his shoulders. To her infinite relief he responded immediately, levering himself above her. One glance at the look of passion shaping his chiseled features and her relief gave way to panic. It was unlike her—very, very unlike her—to let things go this far, and she had no idea how to cool him down.

She started by clearing her throat. "Brad, I'm sorry, but I don't want you to do this."

"Yes, you do," he assured her with easy confidence, bending his head to trail damp kisses along her collarbone.

"No. Really, I can't..." This time her push against his chest was more like a shove. He didn't budge, and Sarah knew the true power of the muscles that made his arms and chest feel like steel girders.

"More *I can'ts* and *I shouldn'ts?*" he teased.

Sarah forced herself to meet his gaze head on. "No, another honest refusal. It's not my fault you're too thick-headed to recognize it as such. Now will you please let me go?"

She held her breath for the full moment it took him to comply. Upon straightening up, he took a long swig of brandy before speaking. "I *must* be pretty thick-headed. And unperceptive. Somewhere along the way tonight, between the tons of questions and that enchanting blush every time I touched you, I got the mistaken impression that you were interested." His eyes captured hers and held them. "Was I mistaken, Sarah?"

"Yes...no..." she sputtered, still rankling from his implication that she was nosy and flustered.

"Surely you can do better than that. I don't particularly enjoy going from a slow burn to a deep freeze without knowing why, you know."

"I told you why. I don't want to. Period."

He arched one brow in interest. "Well, sweet, shy Sarah certainly isn't shy when it comes to saying no, is she? Or when it comes to leading a man on, either."

Sarah could feel a heated blush staining her cheeks and neck a fiery red, but it was anger, not embarrassment, that ruled her tongue. "I never claimed to be shy. Or sweet."

"You didn't have to," he ground out. "Your pal Julie Hazard did it for you. Well, it just goes to show, we all make mistakes. I'm beginning to think my biggest one was in agreeing to Julie's little plan in the first place. The next time someone tells me about her poor, shy friend who hasn't gotten out much since suffering a bad experience with a man, I'll know better than to play Sir Galahad."

Fuming silent oaths about Julie's big mouth, Sarah bounded off the sofa and whirled to glare down at him. "Some Galahad! Just because you made the supreme sacrifice of honoring poor me with your company for the evening, you think I ought to jump into bed with you."

"No, I really think you ought to wait until you're asked." There was something warmly teasing about the smile that revealed a flash of white teeth, but Sarah was beyond being charmed.

Indignation flaring, she lashed back. "You wanted to know if I was interested in you tonight? Okay, I'll tell you. I was interested. Extremely interested. But it was purely professional. By Monday I have to submit to my publisher the names of several candidates for an article we're planning. The only reason I'm here is because Julie insisted you were a prime specimen—and she even got that wrong."

The announcement was like a small explosion in the dimly lit room. Afterward there was only a deathly silence and the myriad emotions flickering across Brad's face. Surprise gave way to confusion and a flicker of irritation before his mouth curved into a thoroughly amused smile, deepening his dimples in a way Sarah found annoyingly distracting.

"I'm glad one of us is enjoying this," she muttered dryly.

Chuckling, he hauled himself to his feet beside her. "I don't think we have much choice. Sarah, it looks like you and I have both been had—by a pro."

"No." She shook her head firmly, but the words "Julie wouldn't do a thing like that" stuck in her throat as she remembered that Julie had a long history of doing things very much like that. In view of Sarah's steadfast opposition to her friend's continual impulse toward matchmaking, Julie would have no qualms about using Sarah's dedication to her job as a subterfuge.

"In fact," Brad continued in a tone of grudging admiration, "right this minute she's probably congratulating herself for killing two birds with one stone."

Sarah shook her head, her mouth curving into a small rueful smile. "I wish I had that stone right this minute. I'd like to tie it around Julie's neck and push her off the Newport Bridge."

"That's a little harsh, isn't it? After all, her plan worked. Aside from the past few moments, I'd say the evening was an unqualified success. Five minutes after I met you I totally forgot I was simply doing a favor for a friend and started enjoying myself. Am I wrong in believing there was a bit of pleasure mixed in with business for you as well?"

Sarah drew a deep breath under his watchful gaze. There was no way she was going to admit to him exactly how greatly pleasure had outweighed business in her mind this evening. Her smile and tone were the epitome of cool control as she said, "Dinner was lovely, Brad, and, as I've already told you, you are a very interesting man. But now that we've both fulfilled our obligations for the evening, I think I'd like to go home."

He received the request with a silence that left her feeling very uneasy as she picked up her purse and moved toward the door. It wasn't until her fingers reached for the brass knob that she discovered how appropriate that feeling was.

"Sarah." She turned to look at him, drawn by the commanding sound of her name on his lips. "We haven't *quite* fulfilled our obligations for the evening. At least I haven't."

Taking her by surprise, he reached out and pulled her close against him. "I feel *obliged* to point out that I did not invite you back here tonight to lure you into my bed. If I had," he continued meaningfully, "I can assure you we wouldn't be standing here discussing it right now."

Sarah would have turned away in chagrin, but the arms gently imprisoning her wouldn't permit it. Even her eyes were held captive by a pair of smoldering green ones ablaze with an awesome male purposefulness that excited and alarmed her at the same time. His voice lowered, becoming almost a drawl.

"I have no intention of seducing you, sweet Sarah. When I make love to you it's going to be because you want it as much as I do. And it's going to be perfect."

Without pause, he swooped to claim her mouth, filling her, taking her with a kiss that was half warning, half promise, and all passion. His fingers glided silkily through her hair as he probed her with lazy thoroughness, then moved his tongue in long, warm strokes that melted any resistance she might have mounted. When he broke away to smile gently down at her, Sarah felt pleasantly ravished and strangely unfulfilled, as if she were suspended over an abyss of pleasures still to come.

"Absolutely perfect," he repeated, his voice slightly hoarse, his meaning crystal clear.

Without replying, Sarah let him lead her out to the car, aware that she should be offended—or at least pretend to be—by such a blatant declaration from a man she hardly knew. Instead, all she felt was warmly glowing and more alive than she had in a long, long time. Tucked snugly into the seat beside him, she swept a glance over the whole appealing length of him and smiled in the darkness. There were probably a thousand good reasons why his smug assumption that they would see each other again shouldn't fill her with a desire that was deeper and sweeter and more precious than any she had ever known. But at the moment, she couldn't think of a single one.

Chapter Three

EYEING THE CARS lined up in front of her, Sarah mentally gauged her chances of making it through the intersection before the light changed. Not good, she decided, nudging the accelerator with a practiced foot to give the aging Chevy just enough gas to keep it from stalling without sending it careening into the late model Mercedes in front of it. She should have taken the side streets home from the office, but who'd have thought traffic would already be stop-and-go at ten o'clock on a Saturday morning?

Cup fever, she sighed, watching clusters of jovial tourists weaving their way through the snarled traffic. It was an indulgent sigh, not a resentful one. Suddenly she was seeing all the hoopla surrounding the America's Cup race in a new light. For that matter, everything seemed a little brighter and more beautiful to Sarah this morning, in spite of the unproductive two hours she had just spent poring over microfilm in the magazine's morgue. As a method of turning up viable candidates for this cursed article, the project had been a dismal failure. No matter what handsome, dashing bachelor she was reading about, the face of one man hung stubbornly before her—a man with smoky green eyes that could laugh or smolder with equal fervor, a man whose face seemed serious, almost stern, until that full smile mellowed it into one that charmed and conquered, a man who danced with loose-limbed grace and kissed with . . .

The not-so-subtle blast of a car horn shocked her back to awareness, and she coasted forward just in time to have the light turn red again. This time she would be ready. Eyes riveted on the light, foot coaxing the temperamental engine to a steady purr, she was startled by a sharp rap on the car window. The young man she'd noticed selling fresh flowers on the corner stood grinning at her, a bunch of daisies in his hand.

"No, thank you," Sarah mouthed through the glass, turning back to the light.

The second rap, coming just as the light turned green, was louder and more insistent.

"I said no," she repeated loudly enough to be heard through the closed window. The idiot just grinned, grabbed the door handle, and motioned for her to roll the window down.

Unable to drive without dragging him along, she shifted her foot from the gas to the brake, promptly stalling the car, and opened the window. Immediately he thrust the daisies at her, prompting her to lift her hand and send them flying back in his direction.

"Are you deaf?" she inquired irritably. "I said I don't want any flowers."

With a shrug he tossed them back into the car, this time aiming for the seat beside her. "Well, want 'em or not, lady, they're yours. They've already been paid for by some guy a few cars back." Amidst the blaring of a long line of car horns, Sarah stuck her head out the window, squinting into the bright sun, as he continued, "That's the one, in the—"

"Black BMW," she finished at the same time.

How had he spotted her? she wondered. She couldn't even see the driver, only a length of black enamel and shiny chrome. However, that was enough to start a curious tension coiling inside her, making it even more difficult than usual to coax old Nellie back to life. When she did get rolling again, she kept darting glances in her rearview mirror, noting each time one of the cars between hers and Brad's turned off.

By the time she'd left the busy wharf area behind and turned onto one of the quiet tree-lined streets that characterized the city's older neighborhoods, only a battered Volkswagen separated them, and it was clear that Brad's presence was not merely coincidental. Pleased beyond reason by that fact, Sarah swung onto Tremont Street and coasted to a stop in front of the gracefully aging two-story structure she called home.

Before she finished collecting the assortment of notebooks and back issues of *Inside Newport* that would comprise her afternoon's reading, Brad's low-pitched "Good morning" slid over her like a velvet glove.

She turned to find him leaning on her car door, arms folded over the half-open window, a beguiling smile shaping the sensuous mouth that had played a major role in her morning daydreams.

"Good morning." She smiled back, absorbing the sight of him, the wind-tousled hair drifting over his forehead, the faded chambray shirt that strained across his broad shoulders and upper arms as he hunched closer. In the paint-spattered shirt, its sleeves rolled up to reveal sun-browned forearms dusted with the same dark hair that peeked from his open collar, he looked very unlike the polished gentleman of last evening, but every bit as appealing.

"Thank you for the flowers." She added the bouquet to the pile of periodicals. "Even if they were the cause of a most embarrassing moment."

His lips twitched slightly in a way Sarah found much

too fascinating. "I couldn't resist—not when I know you have that whole shelf of jelly glasses just sitting there going to waste."

Her attraction to him was a tangible force, elevating her blood pressure and tying her tongue. That he seemed utterly content to stand there, watching her with gentle enjoyment, didn't help inspire a string of witty conversational tidbits. After opening and closing her mouth several times, she finally came out with, "Did you want something?"

A very telling pause followed before the amused smile deepened into something much more compelling.

"It's a little early in the morning for leading questions," he said softly, dipping his head toward her, "but as long as you offered—"

"Hold it." She halted his rapidly descending mouth with a flat palm. Displaying remarkable adaptability, he proceeded to nibble at the soft flesh, teasing it with a deft, tantalizing tongue. "Cut it out," she commanded, chuckling. "That wasn't an offer. It was a polite way of asking you to get out of the way so I could open the car door."

Opening it for her, he swept the stack of notebooks and magazines from her arms and helped her out. "You're good at that, aren't you?" he asked mildly, following her up the porch steps. "Polite remarks, I mean. Do you ever just come right out and ask for what you want?"

"Sometimes," she hedged, studying her key ring closely.

"At work?"

"Yes."

He hitched his shoulder to hold the screen door open while she inserted the key in the ornate lock. His tone remained studiously neutral. "And with men?"

"Boy, you would have made one whale of a prosecuting attorney. Tell me, is the role of interrogator one you're born to, or do they offer it in law school? Grilling, 101 perhaps?"

"Is that your polite way of telling me to mind my own business?" he inquired pleasantly, placing her materials on the hall table.

"That's right, your honor."

With amused surprise she watched as he sauntered into the kitchen with the daisies. The toe of one worn Nike tapped in time to some unheard tune as he filled a jelly glass with water and plunked the flowers in. Then, using his denim-clad thighs as a towel, he strolled back to lean negligently against the wall across from her.

"Anyway, I didn't come here to play twenty questions with you. We can do that later tonight, when I'll have wine and soft music on my side." His dimples made their appearance. "That's my suave and debonair way of asking if you're free this evening."

Before she had a chance to precede her "yes" with a proper pause, he went on, "I realize that dating etiquette, as it has developed through the ages, requires that you inform me that you've already made plans and haughtily suggest that I call earlier in the week next time. But since I didn't know you earlier in the week, and seeing as how I'm willing to commit the single person's ultimate faux pas by admitting I don't have a date for Saturday night, I thought you might be willing to do the same."

He smiled with such absolute confidence that Sarah experienced a fleeting urge to test it by turning him down flat. She did chance a little calculated stalling.

"I hate to tell you this, but suave and debonair you're not. You do have a nice car, though, and I've already seen tonight's TV movie twice." She eyed him critically. "Are you going to wear that shirt?"

"Yes, ma'am." He nodded and added hopefully, "With a plaid tie."

"In that case, how can I refuse?"

"Great. I'll pick you up at seven." He straightened and caught her off guard with a quick kiss. "Make it six." This time the light kiss promised to turn into something delightfully more intense, but the sound of a feminine throat being cleared very loudly intruded.

"May I come in?" Julie asked from the open doorway. "Or were you just warming up?"

Sarah managed to jerk away approximately three inches before Brad's arm, which was resting casually across her shoulders, turned to cement. "Julie, hi. Of course you can come in."

"By all means," Brad echoed dryly, dropping his arm to his side. "Actually, I was just leaving. I'll see you later, Sarah. Good-bye, Julie." He disappeared out the front door, then swung around to add, "And thank you."

"Any time," Julie answered with a magnanimous smile that turned quickly into a frown. "For what?"

Brad's eyes roamed over Sarah in a warm preamble to his reply. "For Sarah, of course."

"For Sarah, of course?" Julie repeated meaningfully after the front door banged shut behind him. An X-rated gleam appeared in her eyes. "When he said he was just leaving, he didn't mean you two had . . . Nah, he couldn't have." Her auburn eyebrows arched in disbelief. "Could he?"

"Of course not." Sarah laughed, shaking her head. "Do you really think I'd ever end up spending the night with a blind date?"

Julie shrugged. "What can I say? I'm an eternal optimist. Hold on before you start delivering lecture fifty-six—the one about how you don't need my help in running your love life. And I use the term love life very loosely," she added, rolling her eyes. "The fact is, we're not talking about just any blind date here. In addition to being gorgeous and sexy and rolling in dough—any one of which could serve as an excuse for indiscretion of an intimate nature—Brad Chandler is just plain nice."

Sarah pondered that while Julie adjourned to the kitchen. She returned with a can of diet soda and flopped onto the couch as gracefully as was possible for a size ten wearing size eight designer jeans.

"If he's so nice," Sarah ventured cautiously, "why haven't you added his scalp to your collection long before this?"

"Precisely because he is so nice. I'd never measure up." Over the top of the can she caught sight of the two bouquets on the end table, and she dropped her tone to a suspicious hush. "Did somebody die?"

Sarah chuckled. "No. They're from Brad."

"See what I mean?" Julie pounced. "He's perfect for you." Clearly anticipating Sarah's protest, she rattled on, "Trust me. I know what I'm talking about. Wasn't I right about his being perfect for your article? If he isn't one of the ten sexiest men in Newport, then I'm a vestal virgin."

Sarah's face was deadpan. "No doubt about it, that makes him one of the ten sexiest. Probably even *the* sexiest." At Julie's offended pout, she added, "Sorry, I couldn't resist."

"You ought to try using some of that ironclad self-control of yours when it counts. It would serve you right if I walked out of here in a huff. And I would in a second, if I weren't dying to hear about last night." The feigned pout melted into an expression of gleeful anticipation. "I don't care what you ate for dinner, so just skip right to the good part."

"You're drooling," stalled Sarah, strangely reluctant to share last night, even with her best friend.

"You're darn right I'm drooling. I want to hear every juicy detail."

Sarah sighed with amused resignation. There was no use trying to appeal to Julie's sense of decorum. When it came to men, she didn't have one. "I hate to disappoint you, but I'm afraid the details aren't all that juicy."

Julie arched her eyebrows again and tossed her long red hair over her shoulders in a no-nonsense gesture. "Ordinarily I might believe that—even expect it. But I don't believe even you could spend the entire evening with Brad Chandler without *something* happening . . . especially given the heartfelt thanks I just got for introducing you."

Sarah's smile was that of a woman with a secret. Something had happened all right. Not the torrid scene Julie was panting to hear about, but something so subtle Sarah herself didn't know yet what it might mean.

"Aha!" shouted Julie, waving her index finger. "I'd know that look anywhere. You have the hots for him."

Sarah had to laugh at Julie's choice of expression. It was one they'd used often when they were roommates in college, back in the days before . . . Sarah's face tightened.

"And I know that look, too," her friend sighed, her voice taking on a softer, more serious tone. "Let it go, Sarah. Rod Whalen was a first-class jerk. He's also something that happened years ago. You can't go on letting a bad experience with one rotten guy turn you off to every man you meet."

"I don't do that." When it looked as if Julie was ready to contradict her, Sarah hurried on. "All right, maybe I have done it in the past, but I'm not doing it now."

Even Sarah was astonished by the absolute truth of her claim. Rod Whalen had been a journalism teaching assistant when she was in graduate school. He was a legend on campus, handsome, charming. Sarah knew it was unthinkable that he'd ever stoop to asking out anyone as unremarkable as she considered herself. Then, one day the unthinkable happened. Rod deigned to sit with her in the cafeteria, and within weeks she'd been swept off her feet and into his well-used bed.

Two weeks later she was just as abruptly replaced by a more attractive model, one who also demonstrated more talent in the sack, Rod had delighted in telling her. For years that cruel rejection had succeeded in reducing her interest in the opposite sex almost into nonexistence. Until now. She knew very little about Brad except that he unleashed feelings in her she wasn't sure she wanted unleashed, that he had a smile that could take her breath away, and that he was not at all like Rod Whalen.

"Really, Jul." She smiled in an attempt to convince Julie. "I know Brad isn't like Rod. For that matter, I'm not quite the naïve pushover I was back then, either. And you were right; I do have the hots for him. Or at least the warms."

She expected the admission to be greeted with a squeal of delight. Instead, Julie looked even more concerned. "Which brings us to major obstacle number two."

Sarah stood abruptly and walked into the kitchen. With transparent diligence she turned the water on full force and began rinsing the few dishes piled in the sink. Outside the window gracefully arching sprigs of forsythia laden with yellow blooms swayed in the mild spring breeze. She wished that breeze could blow away Julie's remark and all the fears and complications it dredged up—the same ones she'd been holding at bay all morning. She wanted the remnants of last night's special glow to remain untarnished as long as possible. Her body trembled slightly as she remembered the way Brad had touched and kissed her.

"You can't just wish it away, Sarah. It's a fact. And it doesn't matter." Julie's words shattered the dreamy memory, turning the warm feeling inside to ice.

"Doesn't matter?" Sarah flung the wet sponge into the sink with a bitter laugh and whirled to confront Julie, her face pinched and tight. "I can never have children. Do you have any idea what that means? How final it is? Believe me, it matters."

Instantly Julie was at her side, placing a protective arm around her shoulders. "Of course it matters. You know I didn't mean it like that." She gave her a hard squeeze. "Remember me? The pesty broad who visited you every day in the hospital? I flunked all my midterms that semester, and I didn't have the good excuse you did."

"You were flunking anyway." Sarah heard herself laugh even as the tears ran salty into the corners of her mouth.

"How indelicate of you to point that out," Julie retorted, handing her a tissue and nudging her into one of the ladderback chairs gathered around the kitchen table. "What I was trying to say is, it doesn't matter in this situation. Don't go putting the cart before the horse. Okay, so you like the guy. That's light-years away from discussing the possibility of offspring."

Sarah propped her elbows on the table and tried to knead away the first traces of a headache. "Don't you see, it's because I do like him that it matters so much. I don't want to start liking him a lot and then tell him about me and face being rejected all over again." Resentment flashed through her, as if it were happening already. "I don't need that aggravation. I have a good job, a good life, lots of friends—I don't need some man ruining all that for me." The resentment melted into dreaminess. "Even if he does have the most beautiful green eyes I've ever seen."

"If you ask me, beautiful green eyes are definitely worth taking a risk for—especially when the face they're in is attached to a body like that." Julie smacked her lips to make Sarah laugh, and she succeeded.

"You're probably right," Sarah agreed, more to placate Julie than from any real change of heart.

"You know I'm right. No, you probably don't, but trust me. This is exactly what you need in your life: a fling with a magnificent hunk of man, a little champagne, a touch of moonlight." She gave an innocent shrug. "And just think, after all my years of attempted matchmaking, you discovered him all by yourself in the line of business."

"Don't hand me that," Sarah countered. "I'm well aware that the business part of last night was just another of your matchmaking schemes traveling incognito." She settled back in the chair with a wistful sigh. "You do make the whole thing sound very tempting though."

"Then succumb. Stop worrying about yesterday and tomorrow, and live for today. When are you seeing him again?"

Sensing she looked extremely cat-that-swallowed-the-canaryish, Sarah replied, "Tonight."

"Hot damn," gasped her friend. "Imagine, my little Sarah with Brad Chandler. It just proves what I always say: No door is truly locked to the man with the right key."

"I've never heard you say that before." Sarah laughed, knowing such a triviality wouldn't bother Julie when she was on a roll.

"Gwen Davies will be green with envy if she gets wind of this. She's been chasing Brad for months." She checked her watch. "And if I leave right now I'll have time to call and tell her before I go to work." She glanced at Sarah uncertainly. "That is, if you're going to be all right."

"I'm fine now. Really. I was just being silly. I promise to take your advice to heart." Sarah walked Julie out the back door onto the airy screened-in porch. The porch was her special haven, one of the things that kept her living in this old Federal period home despite the leaky faucets and creaking floorboards. "I didn't know your show was on Saturdays now."

Julie made a face. "It's not. But Eric Knight needed today off, so"—she slipped effortlessly into her disc jockey voice—"for one time only, WNEW's Saturday line-up will feature the smooth, sexy sounds of Julie Hazard, Newport's queen of the airwaves. Tune me in.

I'll play something special for you." She bounded down the porch steps, stopping at the end of the walk to call back. "And remember, one step at a time. Brad's not going to show up here with a doctor's note certifying him willing and able to contribute to the world overpopulation problem. Let it ride, and make hay while the sun shines, if you get my drift."

Sarah got it. It haunted her all afternoon, and at five o'clock she was still mulling over Julie's advice. Live one day at a time. It certainly sounded like a pragmatic thing to do. But what happened on that day when the good times ran out and the unpleasant truth could no longer be avoided or hidden? Were the days of pleasure worth the heartache that might follow?

Uncertainly she stared at the two outfits she had laid out on the bed. The choice of what to wear for her date with Brad had taken on symbolic importance. Should she wear the sedate blue linen or the gauzy apricot halter with the slit skirt that was guaranteed to knock his socks off?

She paced to her bedroom window to peer through the white lace curtain at the tiny bit of Atlantic Ocean visible in the distance. Instead she saw Brad's face, smiling, his head tilted to one side, eyes crinkling at the corners, dimples furrowed in his cheeks. Just the thought of him sent shivers of excitement racing up and down her spine, and the desire that had been gnawing at her all day mushroomed. Spinning around, she snatched the drab blue dress off the bed and shoved it far into the back of her closet, then went whistling into the shower.

Brad arrived twenty minutes early, with a look so eager it made Sarah's heart sing. His approval of her appearance was implicit in his scorching gaze, and she returned the silent compliment, letting her eyes roam freely over the khaki slacks and navy blazer that fit his hard contours to hand-tailored perfection. After the initial hellos they both stared, quenching the thirst for each other that seemed impossibly strong after only a few hours apart.

"Do you like Italian food?" he asked as he started the car.

"I love it. In fact, you'd have to do some digging to come up with a type of food I don't like."

"I'm glad to hear that. There's nothing more boring than a woman who takes two bites of her meal, then spends the rest of the night talking about the seaweed and grapefruit diet she just started."

Their shared laughter filled the car. "I didn't say I don't diet. After eating pasta in any shape or form I have to do penance the whole following day. But I prefer yogurt to seaweed."

"It doesn't matter," he conceded with a wry smile. "I think I'd even find grapefruit and seaweed a scintillating topic if you were doing the talking." His candid admission thrilled her and left her without a properly casual retort. "And talking about talking," he continued to her relief, "how did Julie's visit go? I expect she wanted a full rundown on last night."

"I see you know Julie better than I thought," Sarah said with a laugh.

"Yes, well, Julie's very nice, but it doesn't take a whole lot of time to zero in on her main area of interest." He accelerated to capitalize on a tight opening that suddenly appeared in the traffic ahead and asked casually, "Did she get it?"

"Get what?" queried Sarah.

"A full rundown."

"Oh, I briefed her on the highlights," she replied with an evasive wave of her hand.

"I'll bet it would be fascinating to compare your version of the highlights with mine. For example, I think the best part of the evening took place after we left my workshop." He flickered a probing glance her way. "Do you agree?"

Sarah averted her eyes, suddenly very interested in peering out the car window. "I don't know. Dinner was nice, and impromptu sidewalk dancing was a whole new experience for me."

"Uh-huh. But *nice* doesn't begin to describe the way I feel when I'm holding you in my arms. And it's been a whole new experience for me to have the memory of a few simple kisses haunt me as it has. You wreak havoc with my powers of concentration, Sarah."

There was a challenge in the husky admission, one Sarah wasn't quite ready to face, let alone accept. She flashed him an innocent smile. "I'd never want to be guilty of that. We'll just have to make sure it doesn't happen again."

"I'm willing to put up with the inconvenience. More than willing."

His eyes deserted the road ahead in favor of her legs, calling attention to a problem he obviously found intriguing. While trying the dress on in the store and waiting for Brad to arrive, Sarah hadn't had occasion to sit down. When she finally did, under his watchful eye, the slit skirt that opened only discreetly when she walked revealed a persistent tendency to slide against the silkiness of her pantyhose, exposing a generous length of thigh. At first she'd determinedly tugged it back into place, then gave up, deciding a little bit of leg wasn't worth appearing neurotic over. All of a sudden, however, more than her mental health seemed to be at stake. Brad's lingering glances made her worry that any moment they might wind up in the trunk of the car in front of them, and she mentally heaved a sigh of relief when he pulled into a parking lot close to the waterfront.

The restaurant turned out to be a small, family-run affair located on the second floor of one of the picturesque old buildings along that part of the waterfront still awaiting the arrival of the city's renewal project. A delicious aroma of mingled spices beckoned them up the narrow wooden stairs to a maze of small adjoining rooms, each holding several tables. With its traditional red-checked tablecloths and candles dripping over straw-covered wine bottles, the interior more than made up in coziness what it lacked in originality.

While Sarah looked on in surprise, Brad tiptoed up to a roly-poly woman standing with her back to them and captured her in an enthusiastic hug. Turning, the woman, who appeared to be somewhere in her fifties, broke into a full smile.

"Brad!" she cried, hugging him back with obvious affection. "So, after weeks and weeks his honor finally remembers his old friends." She pulled away to inspect him from head to toe, shaking her head in dismay as she patted the lean torso beneath his jacket. "Look at how skinny you're getting. When are you going to find a nice wife to cook for you and take care of you?"

Brad smiled, completely at ease. "Whenever you break down and say yes, Anna."

"Bah," she sneered playfully. "I'm not even tempted; you're too skinny." Over his shoulder she glimpsed Sarah and immediately pushed him aside. "Too skinny and no manners. Introduce me to your friend, please."

Sarah allowed Brad to pull her forward, happily cognizant of the pride glowing in his eyes. "Anna, I'd like you to meet Sarah Templeton. Sarah, this is my friend, Anna Rosselini."

Sarah extended her hand, acquiescing gracefully when the older woman instead pulled her close for a friendly hug. "A match made in heaven," she chortled, rolling her eyes in that direction. "You're too skinny, too. Come on. First you'll eat, then we'll talk." She hustled them to a private table by a window, leaving them with two battered menus and a broad wink at Brad.

He dragged his chair around so they were sitting next

to each other and whispered conspiratorially, "I'm afraid she'll insist on knowing your intentions before we leave here tonight."

Sarah played along, crisscrossing her heart with her finger. "They're strictly honorable, I swear."

Brad sighed. "That's what I was afraid of."

Sarah was beginning to enjoy the way his casual teasing was threaded with sensuality, and she turned to peruse the menu with a sense of contentment. When the waitress came to take their order Brad added to her sensibly moderate selections, and Anna ambled over to add to that, so they ended up with a delectable assortment of food that could easily have fed the Rhode Island National Guard. Later, savoring the last morsel of veal with the same appreciation she'd felt for her first bite of the antipasto, she smiled at Brad with a twinge of latent guilt.

"I'll have to eat yogurt for a solid week in atonement, but it was worth it."

"Anna will be pleased," Brad assured her, finding her knee under the tablecloth and the slit skirt and giving it a gentle squeeze.

Anna *was* pleased. And, true to Brad's prediction, she pulled up a chair when she delivered the espresso and launched an inquiry into their friendship, paying little heed to the dictates of polite restraint. Brad fielded her questions with a practiced ease that suggested he'd gone through this routine before, and Sarah knew a ridiculous moment of jealousy thinking that he might have shared his fettuccine Alfredo with some other woman before her. More likely a long string of other women, she chided herself, trying to keep a grip on the reality of the situation between them. It was a real challenge. The combination of the food, the wine, and Brad's lavish attention had her feeling deliciously intoxicated.

She knew he was experienced in the game they were playing in a way she never would be, and yet she had a hunch—or a hope—that his treatment of her was as special as it seemed. Their conversation over dinner had been relaxed and easy, with little of the blatant intimacy he'd suggested in the car. Yet his earlier remarks had set an underlying mood for the evening, a mood kept alive by his frequent light touches and the occasional burning flash when their eyes met. The evening seemed to exist on two levels, one of action and one of anticipation. The heat of the anticipation alarmed Sarah even as it excited her, and she was relieved when Brad suggested they drive to the jai Alai fronton on the other side of the city after leaving the restaurant.

The crowd at the fronton was boisterous, cheering on their favorite players with foot stomping and hand clapping as the *pelota,* or ball, was hurled at speeds of up to one hundred and fifty miles per hour from the wicker baskets strapped to the players' wrists. Sarah and Brad soon discovered a marked difference in their betting styles. She derided his scientific, methodical approach, and he repeatedly tried to convince her not to waste her money on a player just because she liked his name or his legs. Not until the final match, a trifecta, did they decide to combine strategies. After carefully selecting six players on the basis of statistical data, Brad handed her the program.

"All of these have a good shot at winning," he explained. "Now you have to pick the three you like."

Sarah glanced at the circled names, then studied the players sitting and standing around the court.

"Is that really necessary?" Brad demanded with a trace of amused exasperation.

"It is if you want to win," she told him sweetly. "These three."

She put check marks next to their names, and Brad went to place the bet. When the match was over, the winning numbers on the lighted scoreboard were the same as the ones on their ticket.

"You did it!" He caught her to him in a crushing hug.

"You mean *we* did it."

"That's right. We don't make a bad team. From now on we'll work together. I'll check the stats, and you check out the legs." His eyes narrowed in mock warning. "From a distance."

Sarah saluted crisply. "Yes, sir."

"That's what I like, a respectful female." He captured her mouth in a kiss that lasted just long enough for him to flick his tongue playfully across her lips. "And a sweet-tasting one. C'mon, sweet lady, let's go collect our money."

"Forty-two dollars and fifty cents." Brad patted his pocket with an air of satisfaction as they waited in the line of cars snaking its way out of the fronton parking lot. "What should we do with it?"

"Buy a Rembrandt? Take a trip around the world?"

"No, something *really* special. Don't worry, I'll come up with something. I'll dedicate this entire week to thinking about it." His eyes roamed along their habitual path. "Except for those hours I plan to spend being haunted by the memory of your legs in that dress."

"I noticed you noticing," she grumbled, arranging her skirt primly.

"I was sure you did." His smile broadened to a grin as he reached across the seat for her hand.

Driving with one hand, he played the sensitive skin of her palm with his stroking fingers. Conversation lapsed as the soft strains of a romantic ballad filled the car. Sarah fleetingly wondered whether it might be the "something special" Julie had promised to play on her show, but she was soon too distracted to think or even listen. The sensations Brad was creating in her hand spiraled upward and inward, inciting an unfamiliar longing somewhere close to her core. That longing only heightened the sense of anticipation that had cloaked them all evening until, when they finally pulled up outside her house, it was almost a palpable force, sweeping her toward some foregone conclusion.

After releasing it only long enough to turn off the motor and get out of the car, Brad continued to hold her hand all the way up the front walk, surrendering it reluctantly so she could find her key.

"Invite me in for a cup of coffee," he prompted with undisguised hopefulness when her trembling fingers finally produced it.

"I don't drink coffee." Immediately she could have kicked herself for the automatic response. She wanted him to come in every bit as much as his eager expression told her he wanted to. "Would you like to come in for a cup of herb tea?"

His position on the step below her put them on the same eye level. With infinite tenderness he reached up and cupped her face in his hands. "Sarah, sweet lady, I'll come in for a cup of hot water, as long as you understand that what I'm really coming in for is you."

Chapter Four

BRAD SEARCHED HER EYES, apparently reading the hesitant invitation that Sarah suspected was inscribed on them before taking the key from her and unlocking the door. Once inside, she beat an escape route to the kitchen, filling a kettle with hot water and fiddling with the temperamental pilot light on the ancient gas stove. Even without looking she was aware of Brad wandering about her living room, pausing to study the collection of family photographs hanging in a collage-style frame near the fireplace.

"How many brothers and sisters do you have?" he called out, obviously bewildered by the wide assortment of Templetons captured on the wall.

"Three. Two brothers and a sister. The miniature versions in those pictures are my nieces and nephews."

"That's great. Do they all live around here?"

Sarah folded two yellow calico napkins and placed them on a small serving tray. "No. I'm from New Hampshire originally, and they all still live there. We get to-

gether at Christmas and Thanksgiving and once or twice
during the summer."

"You must miss them," he remarked from the curved
archway behind her.

Sarah carefully removed two mugs from the wooden
wall rack without turning to face him. He had no way
of knowing he was traversing sensitive territory. "Mmm.
Although we really don't have that much in common.
Tom and Debby are both doctors, like my father, and
Mark is a research biologist, like Mom." Finally turning,
she flashed him a brief, too-bright smile. "I'm the only
black sheep in the family."

Something flickered in the depths of the green eyes
trained so intently on her face—something that told Sarah
he read the pain beneath her quip—but when he spoke
he wisely let the whole subject drop. "Did you know that
your dress is exactly the same color as the flowers on
the couch?"

"Of course. I bought them as a matched set."

It was a weak joke, but Brad laughed anyway. Aware
that he'd moved closer and was leaning against the kitchen
sink watching her, she painstakingly arranged spoons and
a sugar bowl on the wicker tray.

"Come here, Sarah."

The command was executed in a gentle drawl that
started a curling sensation in her stomach. She was certain if she faced him he would see evidence of it on her
face.

"Just a minute. I want to get the tea ready. Do you
want Cinnamon Zinger or Orange Blossom?"

He drew closer. "Sarah, I hate herb tea."

He hadn't touched her with anything except the heat
of his body, only inches from her back, but the effect
was the same as if his hands had burned over her in an
intimate caress. He lifted the dark, glossy waves at the
side of her neck and replaced them with the warmth of
his lips.

"Maybe you'd rather have a glass of milk." Her voice quivered as he nibbled a sensitive spot she hadn't known was there. "Or a diet soda?"

His hands advanced from her waist to just brush the undersides of her breasts. "You know what I want, Sarah."

Her breathing halted at the passionate longing in his voice. She knew what he wanted: the same thing she wanted. After all, that's what living for the joy of the moment was all about. Except now that push had come to shove, Sarah could feel the bottom dropping out of the philosophy she'd embraced so eagerly just hours ago.

"Please don't be afraid," he breathed close to her ear.

"I'm not." Sarah wasn't sure if that was the truth or the biggest lie she'd ever told.

He shifted to drape one arm around her waist. "Good. Then come over here and sit with me. Talk to me."

Sarah heard in his words the resolve to go slowly, and she was grateful. Still, as she trailed him across the living room, her legs were about as sturdy as a rubber doll's. It was a relief to collapse into a corner of the sofa. Instead of claiming the opposite corner, Brad kicked off his shoes and stretched out full length.

"Do you mind my using you for a pillow?" he asked politely after his head was already settled intimately in the cradle of her hips and thighs.

"No, I don't mind."

He closed his eyes with a contented sigh at the whispered response, a small smile gracing his mouth. Her skirt had slid open with the motion of his head on her lap, and Sarah could feel the silky texture of his hair and the warmth of his neck through her stockings. Taking advantage of his closed eyes, she studied the masculine angles of his cheeks and jaw, the exposed bronzed line of his throat. Her mind was tortured by thoughts of all the things she longed to do: smooth her fingers through his hair, trace the curve of his mouth, steal inside the loosened top button of the blue cotton shirt to discover the feel of the tantalizing fur below. Even more torturous were thoughts of the things she longed to have him do to her.

She knew that with just one touch, one word of encouragement, she could have it all. But these new romantic longings were tempered by the same old insecurities. Was it too soon? Would she be able to fulfill his expectations? What if she didn't? What if she did, and they drew closer? That might be the biggest risk of all.

She seesawed between uncertainty and a heady feeling of expectation, but her carefully constructed defenses were a poor match for the desire his closeness stirred within her. It escalated steadily, and when Brad's eyes slid open, Sarah was sure it was because he had sensed the burgeoning ache palpitating somewhere beneath his head.

"It feels so good just being here with you. It's crazy, but I already feel very much at home." With a wry smile he peered up at her, obviously not at all bothered by the obstacle her lush curves presented. "I have to confess I was looking forward to last night's date with only slightly more enthusiasm than I would a trip to the dentist."

With the tip of one finger he began tracing the V neckline of her dress where fabric met skin, dragging it with breathstealing slowness before skating over her breastbone and treating each rib in turn to a lavish caress.

"I know that in my weaker moments I'm susceptible to Julie's logic," said Sarah, making a gallant attempt to keep up her half of the conversation while everything inside her was slowly melting, "but how did you end up agreeing to squire her charity case friend?"

"Very reluctantly," he admitted, scaling the satiny length of her bare arm with a light touch. "I owed her a favor for plugging my sailing club on the radio, so I was at her mercy. Besides, Julie has a way with words. A few well-placed compliments and she had me convinced

I was the perfect man to help bring you out of your shell."

Sarah's chuckle had a definite huskiness. "I know the feeling. She had me convinced you were the answer to my prayers before I even knew what sort of man I was looking for." She watched laughter infiltrate his smoky green eyes and hastened to add, "For the article, I mean."

"Of course. The article. We never did get around to discussing that last night, did we?" His expression was a study in innocence. "Tell me about this article I'm so perfect for."

Sarah drew a long breath, choosing her words carefully. "It's just a profile on some local men."

He thumb-stroked the soft skin at the inside of her elbow, smiling at the goose bumps that erupted as a direct result. "What sort of men?" The question was distracted but direct.

"Sexy," she replied with deceptive lightness.

Tipping his head back, he grinned up at her with undisguised pleasure, the friction of his hair moving against her thighs an exquisite form of torture. "Thank you. Now, what kind of men is it really about?"

"It's really about sexy men—specifically, the ten sexiest men in Newport."

His brow wrinkled into a frown. "How could I help with a thing like that?" Before she had a chance to point out the obvious, he jerked shocked eyes up to meet her cautious ones. "No."

Sarah bobbed her head. He looked so utterly thunderstruck, she couldn't help smiling. "I'm afraid so."

Sighing, he relaxed back into her lap, burrowing a bit deeper in the process. "I suppose it's a compliment, sort of. I'm just thankful you're the editor and not Julie. Otherwise I might have ended up in the foolish thing."

Foolish had been Sarah's exact word when Miriam had first approached her with this idea. It was also the word she'd used when she described the article to Julie and grumbled about having to scout out suitable candidates. But something in Brad's calm, self-assured assumption that she would bend to his wishes rankled.

"It's not foolish," she informed him flatly. "It's exactly the kind of article that catches people's eye and increases circulation." Thank you, Miriam Blakely. "And my being editor has nothing at all to do with whether you're included in this or any other article."

His eyes probed hers, as if he were trying to determine whether or not she was really serious. Properly concluding that she was, he sat up and swung around to face her. "And what if I asked you not to include me?"

She shrugged and backed herself farther into the corner of the couch—and the argument. "I'd tell you it's not my decision to make. Along with a half a dozen other staffers, I'll simply submit a list of possible subjects at an editorial meeting. The final decision will be a joint effort."

"And you'd go ahead and submit my name even if I asked you not to?"

A sudden thought deepened Sarah's frown. "Would it be detrimental to you professionally?"

"I couldn't care less about how it affects me professionally." With an impatient sweep of his arm he brushed off the one excuse she could have accepted. "Personally, I'd find it very embarrassing, but that's not what I'm getting at. Are you going to submit my name at that damn meeting? Even if I specifically ask you not to?"

"That's my job. And my job comes first."

The angry lines of his face softened somewhat in bewilderment. "How can you say that? I know we haven't known each other long, but—"

"One day," Sarah felt compelled to insert, without knowing why.

"Two, if you want to get technical. But I thought we

felt something that transcended the limitations of time. I know I do." His voice sounded even deeper in its softness.

"That's not the point. I don't make professional decisions based on personal feelings, even ones that transcend time." It was a petty dig, and Sarah could see in Brad's tightened face that it had stung. She braced herself for his retaliation, but after regarding her thoughtfully for what seemed like hours, he only shrugged and forced a fraction of a smile.

"You're right. I was out of line to suggest you do otherwise."

His humble and total capitulation left Sarah with the wind out of her sails and an uncomfortable need to explain. "It's just that my job is very important to me," she offered haltingly. "I've worked hard to get where I am, and I won't jeopardize it all for a casual relationship."

"Who said anything about a casual relationship?" he asked quietly.

Sarah knew what he was trying to say. She read in his earnest expression the willingness to understand. Why wasn't she meeting him halfway? Why had she adopted this ridiculous stance in the first place? And why in God's name was she using it as a wedge against the start of what, only moments ago, had seemed like such a sweet inevitability?

Brad sighed, his mouth quirking in self-amusement. "Well, at least this should bring in a more interesting sort of letter than the usual articles written about me do. Maybe I'll even get a few illicit offers."

The notion of Brad receiving offers, illicit or otherwise, from other women irritated Sarah for reasons altogether different from professional integrity. "I'm glad you've decided to look on the bright side. I'd hate for this disagreement to spoil our . . . friendship."

"Yes, it would be a shame to let anything spoil this

budding friendship," he agreed dryly. The silence lengthened excruciatingly until he finally broke it by standing and slipping his shoes back on. "Well, it's getting late."

"Yes, it is."

The glass-domed clock on the mantel struck midnight, making liars of them both. She wished she had the courage to meet his eyes and laugh, breaking this wall of ice between them. Instead, she followed him to the door, alternately searching the Oriental rug beneath her feet for something clever to say and willing him to say something. Even the classically evasive "I'll call you" would be preferable to nothing.

He opened the door and stopped. "Good night, Sarah. I enjoyed tonight." His lips twisted in a wry smile. "Most of it, anyway."

Without kissing her, without touching her, without hearing her silent pleas, he stepped outside. Sarah stood in the doorway watching him walk away and wishing with all her heart he would turn around. Finally he did.

"You know, Sarah, at the risk of tooting my own horn, I've achieved quite a bit of success in my own field. I started out as a member of a very prestigious law firm; I was the youngest man ever appointed to the state Superior Court. And it's been my experience that all the professional accolades aren't worth a damn on a cold night." The eyes holding hers looked sad, almost disappointed, in spite of his smile. "I wish you better luck."

Easing the door shut, Sarah pressed her forehead against the battered wood and listened as the BMW roared to life. She continued to listen until the sound of the powerful engine gradually faded in the distance. "Nice going, Sarah," she said in a watery voice riddled with self-disgust. "You managed to live one day at a time for exactly six hours and twenty-two minutes."

"I think the awards banquet should be timed to coincide with the kick-off of the preliminary Cup trials.

Don't you agree, Sarah?" Miriam Blakely pushed the oversized horn-rimmed glasses back on her nose and tapped her engraved silver pen on the top of the conference table. "Sarah?"

Sarah shifted uncomfortably in her chair and rejoined the meeting, wondering exactly what she was supposed to be agreeing to. "I think..." she began hesitantly, sending Miriam a silent plea, and a prayer of thanks when she obliged.

"The banquet to formally announce the ten men chosen as the sexiest in Newport," the older woman explained. "Don't you think the week the Cup trials begin is the perfect time for it?"

Sarah frowned. Ah yes, the grand unveiling. At a public banquet no less. This was where she'd taken a mental break from the editorial meeting that was gradually turning a simple feature story into a publicity extravaganza. If Brad had thought it embarrassing to be proclaimed sexy in the pages of a magazine, all this hoopla should give him the thrill of a lifetime. "I don't know, Miriam," she hedged. "That doesn't give us a lot of time to pull things together."

"Nonsense. Sally will supervise and see that everything runs without a hitch. Right, Sally?"

Predictably, Sally, Miriam's girl Friday, nodded enthusiastically and launched into an inspired variation on her boss's "if we all pull together" routine. Sarah divided her concentration between not getting caught daydreaming a second time and wondering if she could possibly slip her list of potential candidates out of the folder beneath Miriam's elbow long enough to ink out Brad's name.

Nodding with feigned interest at Sally's recitation, she silently cursed herself for not following her instincts and leaving him off in the first place. And she probably would have, if Sunday's all-day search for other possibilities hadn't left her two names short of her quota. Julie

was right. She was a poor judge of this particular sweep-
stakes. Even more so since meeting Brad. She'd scanned
page after page of tanned male bodies in tennis shorts,
of classically handsome, supposedly virile men in tuxedoes, without a glimmer of interest. None of them could
hold a candle to the image that seemed seared into some
secret, innermost chamber of her heart.

"As for the men themselves," Miriam said, instantly
capturing Sarah's undivided attention, "I'll have copies
made of these lists of names so you'll each have a chance
to look them over before we take a final vote." As she
spoke she flipped the folder open and thumbed through
the papers inside. "I see Lance Carter is a popular choice."

Sarah was momentarily flustered at the comment about
a local newscaster she had passed over without a pause;
then her heart stopped as Miriam hesitated at a list she
recognized as her own. Arching one thin, blond eyebrow, her boss met her eyes across the table. "Brad
Chandler? Judge Bradford P. Chandler?" she asked with
amused skepticism. Then she flicked the folder shut.
"Who'd have thought of a judge? Well, why the hell
not? I think that shows real vision in this area."

She cornered Sarah on their way out of the conference
room. "Unexpected vision, I might add. How did you
ever come up with Chandler?"

Sarah shrugged. "Oh, just on a whim. Now that I've
had time to think it over, he's probably all wrong for
this."

Before she could follow up with a discreet request
that her list be amended accordingly, Miriam clamped
the folder under her arm and swung off down the corridor
tossing a cheerful, "Time will tell," back over her shoulder.

Retiring to her own office, Sarah spent the afternoon
shuffling papers from one side of her desk to the other
accomplishing exactly nothing. Such inefficiency was
unlike her. She loved her job and did it well, and the

fact that an emotional crisis could send her into such a tailspin was further evidence that she was better off without Brad Chandler messing around in her well-ordered life. That rational observation did not, however, stop her from missing him as if he'd been a part of her life for much longer than a few days. Nor did it stop her from replaying Saturday evening over and over in her mind with a variety of more satisfying endings.

Turning her back on the discouraging mess of work before her, she stared out her office window. The headquarters for *Inside Newport* was a stately old Victorian mansion sitting high on a hill overlooking the harbor. Sarah's corner office afforded her a bird's-eye view of the bustling activity around Bannister's Wharf and the stretch of sailboat-dotted blue water beyond. But the scene she'd once found so picturesque now only jarred memories of Brad and encouraged her miserably accurate hindsight.

During the tossings and turnings of the long night that had followed Brad's departure, she'd admitted that her obnoxious defense of her career arose out of some misguided fear. It was a theory Julie had long championed and Sarah had long denied, but now that fear, which formerly had insulated her from what she didn't want, was costing her something she wanted very much, and the time had come to face it.

With that firmly in mind, she spent Tuesday reassuring herself that if Brad did call again, she would be ready with an apology and the resolve to take things as they came. By Wednesday she'd progressed to toying with the idea of calling Julie, confessing how she'd managed to botch things, and seeing if a "chance" meeting might be within Julie's power to arrange. She fought the impulse, but by Thursday morning she was losing the battle, and a hint of pessimism was beginning to color her hope that Brad was missing her as much as she was missing him. It was in a mood of hopelessness bordering on desperation that she tore herself away from her back-logged work to answer the phone just before noontime.

"Sarah Templeton," she said crisply into the receiver that suddenly turned into a block of ice in her hand at the sound of the deep rough-velvet voice she now heard even in her sleep.

"Sarah Templeton, I think that is the most direct, cut-and-dried thing I've ever heard fall from your beautiful lips."

He wasn't angry! In fact, he sounded decidedly warm and friendly. The thought filled her world with sunshine. "Brad, it's nice to hear from you. I was hoping you'd call so I could apologize for the other night."

"That's not necessary, Sarah," he said softly, his voice pouring from the phone to caress her ear and tingle a direct path to her heart. "We both got a little hot under the collar over something that really doesn't matter."

"It does matter. I was so engrossed in what I had to do, I didn't even stop to consider your feelings. After-ward I realized I'd be just as uncomfortable being in-cluded in an article about the ten sexiest women in town."

"But infinitely more worthy of the honor."

The low-key praise left her biting her lip and smiling into the receiver.

"Let's just drop the whole subject," he continued. "You have a job to do, and I had no right to interfere."

"Of course you did," she protested. "After all, you do have a personal stake in this. I can imagine how embarrassing it would be for a man in your position to be included in something like this, and I wish I'd had the sense to listen to you the other night."

His chuckle was a deep-pitched burst of warmth. "My position, as you put it, has nothing to do with it. And it certainly had nothing to do with the other night. I was acting like a spoiled kid, trying to get you to do what I wanted just to prove something I had no right to expect you to prove. Yet."

Sarah ignored the qualifier, which promised things she was still shy of exploring. "Maybe you'll get lucky and not be chosen."

He groaned loudly. "At this point I think that might be even worse for my ego than being chosen. I should probably let you go so you can rally support for me there at the office, but before I do I want to tell you how I spent the morning."

"Handing down wise and profound decisions from your lofty bench?"

"Uh-uh. Something even more important—frittering away the money we won at jai alai."

"Am I the lucky owner of a new mink coat?"

"No, you're the recipient of an invitation to dinner. Tonight. Here at my place. How lucky that makes you remains to be seen."

After she explained that she often walked to work, he arranged to pick her up at the office. She hung up basking in a glow of anticipation that kept her walking on air all afternoon.

By the time they reached his place that evening, her happiness had skyrocketed to giddy proportions.

"Let me have your jacket, and I'll hang it up," instructed Brad, helping her out of the ivory linen suit's bolero jacket. She watched in amusement as he slung it over a hook on the hall tree, pleased to see his notion of "hanging it up" mirrored her own. Walking back to her, he placed his hands on her shoulders and steered her toward the kitchen with teasing determination. "Your job is to sit and keep me entertained while I put together this feast."

She was summarily deposited on one of the stools at the counter separating the galley kitchen from a dining nook. The small round table had been covered with a cream-colored cloth and set with what Sarah suspected was painstaking care, complete with china, crystal, sesame breadsticks in a narrow basket, and a single red rose dead center.

"Sip this while you observe a master at work." He set a glass of white wine before her. "I'm going to see to it that you relax tonight, even if I have to resort to the demon alcohol to accomplish it."

"That won't be necessary. I'm already relaxed," she informed him laughingly, surprised at how true that was. She felt none of the slightly gnawing tension she had experienced on their previous dates. Somehow, since their phone conversation she felt totally at ease with him. Just the fact that he had called imbued her with a certainty that he felt some of what she was feeling and left her blessedly free of worry about where it all might lead.

Propping her chin in her hands, she examined the array of vegetables lined up on the kitchen side of the counter— celery, mushrooms, and several she knew she'd never seen at the local supermarket. "Are you by any chance a closet vegetarian?" she asked.

"Not by a long shot," he chuckled, chopping away with an abandon that made Sarah drop her hands to the safety of her lap. "Up until a couple of weeks ago I thought a parsnip was just a white carrot, but a friend of mine is taking a course in Oriental cooking, and she got me interested."

Sarah overcame the urge to ask how good a friend this friend was. "What are you making?"

"Scallops with julienne vegetables, I hope. This is the first time I've tried any of this." He accompanied the slightly sheepish admission with a nod at the stainless steel wok nearby. "But I've watched Nancy do it twice, and it looks like there's nothing to it. Especially for a great team like us."

Sarah smiled gamely, loath to admit the extreme limitations of her cooking ability and determined that anything this Nancy could do she could do better. "It looks good so far."

"All this chopping is the toughest part. The actual cooking goes much more quickly." Halting mid-chop, he squinted at the vegetables with a look of concern. "I think I'm supposed to be heating the oil while I'm chopping the bok choy."

Sarah was on the verge of pointing out that, as far as she was concerned, if the bok choy was that elongated cabbagelike thing next to the mushrooms he could skip it altogether, when he returned to make quick work of it with his knife, deftly transferring everything to the heated wok. Fascinated, she watched as he swirled the vegetables with chopsticks, pushing them high on the wok's sloped sides as they finished cooking, all the while keeping up a steady and surprisingly informed narrative on the technique of stir-frying. When the vegetables had reached a crisp-tender state he declared perfect, he sprinkled the scallops with lemon juice and cooked them in the same manner. Refusing to permit Sarah to lift a finger, he volleyed between the sizzling wok and the rice steaming on the stove and finally brought it all to the table with a boyish pride that was unconsciously disarming.

"It's delicious," she raved after managing to capture the first bite with the chopsticks he insisted were required.

"You could at least have the tack not to sound so amazed," was his grumbling retort, but he was obviously pleased by the praise. And a bit relieved, Sarah noted with amazement.

She spent the next few minutes chasing a piece of celery around and around her plate, glancing up to find him watching her with an expression that bordered on enchantment.

"I think you have in your possession the most potent

diet aid ever discovered," she said, feeling inordinately self-conscious. Her voice slightly breathless, she waved the chopsticks. "At the rate I'm going, I'll fall asleep before I can overeat."

With a sympathetic chuckle he deftly captured a scallop with his chopsticks and leaned across the table. "Let me help."

For the twenty-eight years preceding that moment, eating had been a necessity for survival, often enjoyable, occasionally sublime, but never the wholly sensuous experience it became under Brad's mesmerizing gaze. His own lips parted slightly as she leaned forward to accept his offering. She chewed slowly, then licked her lips, and all the while their eyes clung, his ablaze with a hunger that clearly had nothing to do with the plate before him.

"Maybe I should just go on feeding you." He lifted another scallop from his plate, but Sarah shook her head.

"I wouldn't want your bok choy to cool off."

A teasing smile lifted the corners of his mouth, and her heart along with it. "I challenge anything to cool off around here tonight."

"It does seem highly unlikely," Sarah agreed softly, delighted to see his dark eyebrows lift a fraction in what looked like pleased surprise. A hunger that was a match for his streaked like wildfire through her veins as she lowered her eyes to her plate and with studied casualness asked, "Where does one go to buy bok choy these days, anyway?"

His laughter had a full, rich sound that appealed to her greatly. "The Oriental market over on Claiborne Street, when they have it. I had to stop in yesterday morning and again today to get it."

"A real hot item," she concurred solemnly. Then she halted her chopsticks in mid-air to eye him suspiciously. "Yesterday and today. What do you do, call a recess so you can catch up on your marketing? What an exposé this would make! Just think, this could launch me into a whole new career—investigative journalism. Tell me, your honor, exactly how many hours a day do you public servants serve?"

He returned her grin. "Speaking only for himself, this public servant is forced to admit that he currently serves exactly none."

While she was still gaping, trying to decide if his suddenly serious expression was legitimate, he continued.

"As of this past Monday, I am officially on a leave of absence."

"Should I ask why?"

His dimples reappeared briefly. "I'd be crushed if you didn't." Then, with a slightly awkward shrug, he volunteered, "It's what I've wanted to do for a long, long time, but it took something you said the other night to bring it all into focus for me. You asked me if I got as excited over my work as a judge as I do over my sailboats. The answer has always been a resounding no, but I've avoided and ignored and rearranged the simple facts of the matter for years. Hearing you put it so directly was like having one of those comic book lightbulbs flick on over my head."

He reached out to stroke her cheek with the back of his fingers. "Don't look so stricken. I'm not quite enough of a free spirit to toss my whole career away overnight. Hence the leave of absence. I figure if I can't make up my mind inside of the next thirty days, I deserve to spend the rest of my summers sweltering in those damn black robes."

"But how will you live?" she asked, giving full rein to the curiosity bubbling inside. "Sailing is a hobby, not a money-making occupation. You'd have to win a lot of races to keep this place going."

"Money isn't an issue," he said bluntly. "As it is, my judge's salary doesn't come close to supporting what you call a hobby and what my parents insist on terming an addiction. I could easily live on the investment income that finances my sailboats. And racing isn't what I plan on doing. I want to continue to design my own boats and eventually expand production to sell to the public."

Enthusiasm laced his tone as he recounted how fellow sailing enthusiasts had been asking him for years to design and build boats for them. In modest terms he spoke lovingly of the boats he'd built and of all the innovative new ones he couldn't find time to get off the drawing board, much less into the water. Sarah learned that Newport was one of the top three markets in the country for the sort of pleasure craft he planned to produce, and that he had a friend, an older man named Joe, who owned a shipyard and had offered to rent him the space he'd need to get started. She also learned that the dimple-flashing smile appeared regularly when he spoke of his dream.

"So what do you think?" Brad asked finally, drawing a deep breath and holding it while he waited for her reply.

"I probably should feel a little guilty for the part I played in what might well be your desertion of a very noble profession."

"But?" Brad prompted, reading her so perfectly he was already breaking into a smile.

"But I don't feel even one little twinge of guilt. I think it's terrific. Stupendous. The most exciting thing I've ever heard. And if you could see your face when you talk about it, you wouldn't need even thirty hours to make up your mind."

The breath he'd drawn so long ago seemed to explode from deep within his lungs. "You don't know how much I needed to hear you say that. After our run-in Saturday night, I was almost afraid to call you, even though you were instrumental in my decision. I wasn't kidding when I said you haunt me. I see your face in the mirror when I brush my teeth. I laugh at your jokes even when I'm alone. You boggle my mind, Sarah. And I was afraid that on top of everything else right now, I wouldn't be able to handle you. The last few days proved to me that what I can't handle is being without you."

"I know the feeling well," she said softly, reaching across the table and covering his hand with hers. For a minute he seemed to savor her gentle pressure. Then, with a flick of his wrist, he caught her hand tightly in his.

"Being with you just might be the most important thing in my life right now. Knowing that you support me, that you don't think I'm tilting at windmills, is just the icing on the cake." He gave her hand a squeeze. "But please keep it up. I have a feeling that, outside of other sailing nuts, you are going to comprise my entire cheering section."

"Your parents?" she began quizzically.

"Are not worth discussing tonight." He kissed her hand, studying its smooth surface as if it were a precious work of art. "Suffice it to say that they will be displeased, maybe enough so to prompt a trip back here. Which might be a blessing in disguise. At least they'd get to meet you. I'd travel twelve hundred miles for that privilege any time," he murmured between lips busy seducing the inside of her wrist with sensations unlike any she had ever known.

"Really?" She took advantage of the position of her fingers to tickle him under the chin, discovering it was an extremely vulnerable spot. "How far would you travel for the privilege of doing the dishes?"

"That's not fair." He jerked his neck out of reach of her fingers.

"Okay, I'll make it up to you," purred Sarah. "You cooked, so I'll wash."

"Sounds reasonable." He nodded like a man who makes his living looking wise and thoughtful.

"And you can dry." Disengaging her hand, she shot

from the seat and was stacking dishes by the sink when he came up behind her.

"Why do I have the feeling I just got taken? And why am I loving it so much?"

The teasing questions thrilled Sarah as no flowery compliment could have. She was actually flirting. And successfully. The heady feeling that resulted was like having a magic wand waved over her. The ivory linen slacks and pale lilac blouse might have been a Paris original for how beautiful she suddenly felt in them. Elbow deep in dishwater she felt inordinately elegant, even sexy. And Brad's raking glances told her she wasn't alone in her estimation.

The aura deepened as they washed and dried and bantered in a way that was a preamble for one thing only. Brad made numerous forays into the soapy water, complaining about her slipshod dishwashing and seizing the opportunity to fish for her hand. Their eyes met time and again in a way that brought smiles to both of them, smiles that lingered even after they dragged their attention back to the task at hand. They dallied over it, as though it were an intricate, very necessary ritual that soothed even as it sharpened anticipation to a razor's edge.

Sarah finished rinsing the last plate and started putting away the ones he'd finished drying. Following his directions, she opened drawers and cabinets, loving the domestic intimacy involved in learning the arrangement of his kitchen.

"Serving platter?" she inquired, holding it aloft.

"Last cabinet on your right, top shelf, but you're going to need some help getting it up there." He slung the dishtowel over his shoulder and crossed the room, but instead of taking the platter as Sarah expected, he grasped her waist from behind and lifted her in the air. "How's that?"

His words were a warm gush of sensation close to her ear, making her hands on the platter tremble revealingly.

"Fine. No, a little higher, please."

"Better?"

"Uh-huh," she mumbled, lucky to get even that out. He'd moved her higher all right, and closer, too, so that the side of his head brushed her hip. "All set."

He let her slide back down, slowly, so she could feel every warm, powerful inch of him against her back. When her feet touched the floor his hands stroked upward from her waist to her neck, smoothing the muscles there with a light touch.

"You're relaxed." There was surprise in the observation. "I expected you to be a bundle of nerves."

It was true. She was relaxed, confident in her ability to let the evening unfold naturally and miraculously free of the uneasiness she'd thought was unavoidable at such a moment. It was a miracle she wasn't about to question. Turning in response to his slight pressure on her shoulders, she met the masculine desire blazing in his eyes and felt its counterpart rocket through her.

"I don't think I've ever seen that smile on you before." He traced it with a slightly rough fingertip, his own mouth curling up at one corner. "Whatever could you be thinking about?"

"About your gourmet taste," she confided, thrilling to the age-old chase, obeying the urge to touch his lips in turn.

He licked her finger, lowering his head and murmuring, "My thoughts exactly."

"I meant in food." She halted his descent and let her gaze rove over his shoulder to the groceries on the counter beyond. "Croissants from Bailey's, orange marmalade, freshly ground coffee—quite a step up from Goofy Grape."

Brad glanced at the counter, then back at her, looking part conquering hero and part little boy caught with his hand in the cookie jar. "It's not my usual fare, but I thought a romantic dinner like ours should be followed by a breakfast of the same caliber."

His voice was low, husky, his eyes on fire with all the emotions she was feeling, and time seemed to stop around them. "How do you feel about croissants in bed?"

Chapter Five

THE QUESTION SHOOK Sarah's newfound confidence to its tenuous roots, and Brad smiled tenderly at her sudden stillness. His dark eyes held more than desire; there was an invitation in their smoky depths. An invitation Sarah knew was hers to accept or decline, now, before sensation overruled caution, coaxing a surrender that might be regretted at some future, saner moment.

In musing silence he watched her, their only point of contact his fingers on the sides of her throat, moving in a slow, random caress she felt all the way to her toes. Why had she never realized what a highly erogenous zone that was? she wondered. Probably because it never had been until it knew the magic of his touch. Closing her eyes, she savored the wonder of it, seeing with new clarity the benefits of living for the joy of the moment. Confidence returned in a warm rush, filling her with a sureness that had nothing to do with tomorrow or with yesterday, but only this glorious moment.

She lifted the curtain of her lashes and smiled up at

him, saying nothing. It was enough. He caressed her back through the silk blouse and pulled her close to the solid wall of his chest. His fingers tangled in the shiny layers of her hair, tipping her face up to meet his firm mouth in a kiss that tasted of relief and impatience mixed in a dizzying, tantalizing meld of lips and tongues. He drew back just a bit, leaving her breathing in short, shallow gulps, and the breath she took in was his. The intimacy of it rocked what was left of her cautious nature and sealed her fate.

Sarah would have guessed it impossible for him to navigate the narrow spiral staircase with her in his arms, but he managed admirably. She felt small and fragile cradled against his strong body, her cheek tucked close to the place where his heart thundered a tempo that echoed her own. Reaching the loft, he gently lowered her to her feet on the braided rug that covered the polished plank floor. He touched a wall panel to dim the lights throughout the house, leaving only the illumination coming from the stained glass mural mounted on the wall over his bed. Recessed lighting filtered through the intricately pieced glass, forming a kaleidoscope of hazy color on the midnight-blue coverlet, imbuing the loft with a soft, rosy glow.

"This is beautiful," Sarah whispered, lifting her fingers, hovering over his shirtfront tinged pink from the light, finally making the tentative contact that earned her a heartstopping smile from Brad.

He shook his head deliberately. "No. You're beautiful." His voice was soft, deep, more stirring to the woman in his arms than a full symphony. "Unbutton my shirt, Sarah."

She longed to appear calm, at ease, but it was hard to fight the habits of a lifetime. She'd always dreaded tackling new things in front of an audience, even an audience of one. And undressing a man definitely qualified as a premiere performance. Nothing in her limited experience had prepared her to take even that active a role in lovemaking.

Her fingers moved tentatively, fumbling over the first button. The next few were liberated with growing ease and curiosity, and she barely hesitated at all before tugging his shirt free of the faded denims to fully expose his broad chest to her searching eyes.

"Touch me." It was part plea, part command, tangled in a husky growl.

Eagerly her fingers obeyed. She closed her eyes and let her fingertips absorb the warmth of his skin, the firm, unfamiliar feel of the muscles layered beneath the smooth surface. She let them wander through the soft, thick wedge of dark hair, tracing it with indrawn breath as it narrowed to a silky line before disappearing into his snug jeans. She sensed him holding his breath as she lingered in that explosive region before she lost courage and stroked upward again.

Sarah knew her own breath was coming far too quickly. A host of sensations, all of them new, swept over her as he covered her hands with his and guided them to the edges of his open shirtfront, then helped her ease it off his shoulders and over his arms. As it fluttered to the floor he pulled her against him and lowered his head. His mouth moved over hers, angling for the perfect fit. Once found, his tongue swept across her lips, pressing lightly, coaxing secrets she was eager to share. She parted her lips for him and met his tongue with the warmth of her own. They took turns probing, sliding against and into each other until, with a deep groan, Brad seized complete control, thrusting into her mouth with long aggressive strokes, swamping her with spasms of wild delight.

The kiss ended with the same intensity. He tore his lips from hers to blaze a trail of hot, licking kisses along the side of her neck, murmuring husky words of approval between labored breaths. Moving his hands slowly, he caressed her back and the full curve of her hips until she felt intoxicated by the sheer pleasure of his touch. A frustrated oath escaped him as his searching lips encountered the silky barrier of her blouse. His dark head lifted, and his eyes, glittering green in the soft light, watched his hands coasting over her breasts. Shivers of delight coursed through Sarah, but the shivers turned to trembling when his fingers lifted deliberately to the top button of the lace-edged blouse. He couldn't help but feel the instinctive response, and his eyes slid up to search hers, his hand frozen in place.

In a deep whisper he asked, "Sarah, how long has it been for you?"

The query was delicately vague, but pretending to not understand was out of the question. "A long time," she said simply. "A very long time."

His awed smile was a surprise. She'd thought her inexperience would have been painfully obvious long before now. "That makes tonight even more special. I'm honored."

She flashed him a nervous smile. "That may be a little premature. My experience was not only long ago"—she cleared her throat softly—"it was also sort of . . . limited."

He seemed to be fighting to keep the corners of his mouth from curling. "That's not a crime. And I think it answers another question I had. I was going to ask if you're protected."

Sarah felt her muscles contract in sequence, like crazed dominoes. Her mind reeled in confusion. For obvious reasons the thought had never occurred to her, but how to explain that at such a moment escaped her. "I don't . . ."

His hands moved to her face, slightly calloused thumbs smoothing over what were probably worry lines on her forehead. "It's okay," he murmured soothingly. "I'll take care of it. And you. Let me take care of you, Sarah. Let my love erase everything that's happened to you before tonight. Let me make you feel as special and new as you've made me feel."

His deep voice flowed over her like a blanket of security. She felt tension ebbing as his fingers began a slow, sensuous dance over her body, seeking out secret places that thrilled to life at his touch. Standing on tiptoe, she wound her arms around his neck and pulled him down to meet her waiting lips. She practiced what he'd taught, tracing his lips with the tip of her tongue, transferring her moisture to him before capturing his tongue with a soft suction that tightened as his hands tugged her blouse free of her waistband and slipped inside to brand the soft skin of her back.

"I'm going to take you slowly." His words were a husky whisper against her parted lips. "As if it were the first time. And in a lot of ways it will be."

This time when she trembled against him it was from hunger, and when he lifted her to the bed, her need matched the one flaming bright in his eyes. Her veins throbbed with it, making the short wait while he shed his jeans seem an eternity.

It was almost worth waiting an eternity. In the soft shadows he seemed to Sarah a bronzed image of perfection. He approached her without a trace of self-consciousness, and she watched the same way, thoroughly mesmerized, as if this first sight of him might be her last. His shoulders looked even broader as he loomed over her, his body longer, leaner. Her eyes traveled over him eagerly, the woman in her instinctively relishing all that was male in him: the muscular angles of his arms, his narrow hips, that dark curling mat that turned silky over his flat belly only to thicken again around the proud evidence of his arousal.

He bent slowly, touching his open mouth to hers with increasing intimacy as the mattress dipped beneath his weight. The sparks ignited by his kiss turned to flames that caused a sweet, slow melting somewhere deep inside 'her. When she wrapped her arms around him, running her fingers up and down his spine, he arched against her with a barely controlled passion that made her shudder.

Misreading her response as fear, Brad immediately rolled to his side, keeping her pressed close against him. "Don't be afraid, Sarah. I'll make it so good for you. I promise."

"I'm more concerned about making it good for you," she admitted softly in a courageous moment of honesty.

His low chuckle tickled the ear he was busy nibbling. "I don't think that ranks as a concern at all. Just being with you is good for me. And I have all night to make you happy." His warm tongue slid lower, teasing the pulse point at the base of her throat. "Although that may prove superfluous. Judging from that last kiss, I'd say you have considerable natural ability in this area, even if you are a little improperly dressed for it." He drew back, searching her eyes for a reaction to his fingers toying with the tiny pearl button near her neck. "May I?"

Her small nod sent his fingers moving over the loop buttonholes. They proved to be only slightly more expert than her own. "Whoever heard of making buttons this small?" he grumbled impatiently.

"I could help."

"Not a chance." His voice was playfully gruff. "This pleasure is all mine. But if you're looking for something to do with your hands..."

Interrupting his task momentarily, he guided Sarah's hands to his chest, sighing his approval when she began moving them in a way she hoped would please. She explored the hairy terrain with growing abandon, stopping to gently rub his flat nipples, smiling in wonder when they obliged by hardening in response. It was almost an annoyance when he interrupted to slide her blouse off. Her slacks followed, dealt with in a manner that was just expert enough and just clumsy enough to put her totally at ease. When she was clad only in the lacy orchid camisole and matching panties, he eased her back on the pillows and gazed down at her with a smoldering approval that said more than words ever could.

Eager to feel every inch of his skin against hers, Sarah raised her arms in a silent invitation he accepted instantly. For a long moment he supported his weight on his elbows, teasing her with the light brush of his chest against her thinly veiled nipples, which were rapidly tautening.

Then his mouth dipped to cover hers in a slow, full possession that was only the first movement in a sonata of sensuous touches and techniques that left her unable to think of anything except the hands and mouth exploring her with such tender expertise. Her flimsy underthings were done away with in a burst of hunger, freeing the fullness of her breasts first to the caress of his passion-clouded eyes, then his gently stroking fingers, and finally the sweet ministrations of his mouth. His tongue flowed over the soft mounds with meticulous care, leaving a faint sheen of moisture in its wake. Unhurried, never faltering, he moved from one breast to the other, licking, gently sucking, until the tips hardened and stood out like rubies against her honey-toned skin.

While Sarah's hands traversed his broad back, seeking to know every inch of him within her reach, his stroked lower, touching her belly and thighs in new ways, ways that pleased and excited, until at the end of that very circuitous route his fingers found the treasure they sought and entered. His hoarse groan mingled with her soft cry, and when their eyes met, Brad smiled.

"You're ready now, Sarah," he said low, close to her ear. "But I want you to be more than ready. I want you to want it more than the air you're breathing."

With patience and adoration he made that happen, bringing her to a height of pleasure beyond her wildest imaginings. She lost herself in the heady sensation of skin sliding against skin, in a universe that began and ended with his velvet touch and huskily whispered words of praise. The curling sensation at her center grew more urgent, becoming a gnawing ache that intensified until she gladly would have bartered her next breath for fulfillment. Heeding her soft cries and the frantic arching of her hips, Brad braced his hands by her shoulders and covered her body with his.

His possession was not as painful as her first time, nor as painless as Sarah had expected. Tight muscles yielded slowly to the steady, patient strokes he accompanied with soothing whispers of encouragement. That he continued to reassure her and rein his own passion to her slower pace, even when his labored breathing revealed the effort it was costing him, caught at Sarah's heartstrings and bound them firmly in Brad's possession. Then she slipped beyond hearing, beyond thinking, spinning in a blizzard of white-hot sensations and wild desires that exploded in the last furious thrusts before he surrendered his own incredible control and slipped with her over passion's edge.

As if some delightful anesthesia were wearing off, feeling seemed to return to Sarah from her toes up. It wasn't peppy get-up-and-go feeling, but a delicious lassitude that contradicted everything she'd ever read about women feeling chatty afterward. She chuckled at that.

"What's so funny?" Brad sounded about as energetic as she felt. He'd rolled off, still holding her close, and now his chin scraped against the top of her head with each word.

"I was just remembering how sex manuals always say that women like to talk after...afterward. And I can't think of anything significant enough to say."

"Hmmm." His thoughtful sigh ruffled the wispy curls near her temple. "Words do seem a bit anticlimatic at a time like this. Maybe we should sing."

She angled her head to send a curious gaze his way. "You're crazier than I thought. And to think, every day you hold people's futures in your hands."

"I'd rather hold you in my hands every day," he growled with decided increase in spirit.

Sarah smiled and planted a string of quick kisses along his chest. "Brad," she began hesitantly, "I didn't . . . That is, what happened tonight never happened to me before."

"I know." His deep voice held all the understanding and reassurance she would ever need.

"If we do it again, do you think it could ever be this good?"

He laughed softly, pulling her even closer. *"When* we make love again, I guarantee it will be every bit as good." With one smooth motion he rolled flat on his back with her sprawled on top of him. "Of course I should warn you that if we keep this up, I'll probably die young"— he flashed her a tantalizingly wicked grin—"but very, very satisfied."

The following afternoon Sarah sat staring out her office window at a sun-sparkled Newport harbor, happily ignoring the work piled eyebrow high on her desk. She'd done little except stare out the window and answer an occasional telephone call since she'd arrived at work three hours late.

Although she was alone, a scarlet hue invaded her cheeks at the memory of how those three hours had been spent. She'd awakened to find Brad lying on his side watching her, his chin propped in his hand, the sheet a tangle of white bunched about his hips. His good-morning kiss had been a leisurely eye-opener, and while her half-awake brain was still reeling from it, he'd informed her she was already twenty minutes late for work, dialed her office number on the bedside phone, and handed it over to her saying, "Now repeat after me . . ."

In the nick of time she'd composed herself enough to speak coherently and change his laughing "I'm stuck in bed" excuse to "I'm stuck in traffic."

Of course when she'd finally arrived, after a quick stop at her place to change clothes, she'd had to answer all those stupid questions about where she'd found a phone in the middle of a traffic jam, and what kind of traffic would make such a short drive take three hours anyway, but it was worth it. Every glorious one of the hundred and eighty minutes had been worth it. Brad was worth it, she decided, worth whatever risk and worry might be involved in their relationship. Why hadn't she listened to Julie long ago? A sudden thought cut short Sarah's languorous stretch. No, thank God she hadn't listened long ago, for until very recently her life hadn't been blessed with the incredible wonder of Brad Chandler.

A perfunctory knock preceded her secretary Melanie's entrance. "Sarah, have you forgotten the editorial meeting with Mrs. Blakely at two?" she asked, taking a step closer to examine the towering pile of papers on the desk. "Not to mention this Sorenson contract and these photos of the surfing tournament that were supposed to be in Harvey's hot little hands before noon. What have you been doing closed up in here?"

Sarah ignored the question and the fact that she would have to come up with some excuse to pacify Harvey, the magazine's talented but temperamental photography editor. Scrawling a brief note, she clipped it to the contract and handed it to Melanie along with the top four photos from the pile in front of her. "So much for all that. Now for the meeting. Is Miriam waiting in the conference room?"

"With bated breath, along with the rest of the staff," Melanie replied, tossing her boss a sympathetic smile.

Sarah darted a glance at her watch and bolted for the door, muttering under her breath.

"Relax," Melanie called after her. "You've never been late before. Unless you count those three hours this morning, of course."

Sarah couldn't spare the two seconds to turn and direct a withering glare at her secretary, but the delivery boy she passed on the stairs took pains to get out of her way quickly. She reached the conference room adjoining Miriam's third-floor office and pushed the door open to be greeted by five pairs of very curious eyes.

"Sorry I'm late," she said, slipping into a seat at one end of the long table. "What did I miss?"

"Just Brenda's home remedy for removing ink stains from silk and ten minutes of my impatient foot tapping," Miriam informed her, lifting a hand to forestall any explanation. "Never mind the excuses; let's just get this show on the road. Sally, have you received permission from the Historical Society to hold the banquet at the Marble House yet?"

Sally nodded and launched into an in-depth explanation of how the mansion on Newport's famous Bellevue Avenue would be arranged for that evening, including information about the band, the menu, and miscellaneous details right down to the color of the table linens. Sarah listened with as much enthusiasm as she could muster for this extravaganza. More than ever she was seeing the whole thing through Brad's eyes and regretting her decision to nominate him more with each word Sally uttered. Beneath the table she superstitiously crossed her fingers in the hope that Brad would not turn out to be anyone else's idea of overwhelmingly sexy.

The chances of that were infinitesimal. To Sarah it seemed obvious that Brad gave new meaning to the words *masculine* and *virile,* and she couldn't imagine the astute group gathered around her not picking up on it. No doubt about it, she thought miserably, Brad was about to be proclaimed one of the ten sexiest men in Newport. Now all she had to worry about was finding a tactful way of letting him know how much publicity and hoopla would go along with that dubious honor.

"Now for the good part." Miriam's intentionally bawdy

tone drew Sarah's complete attention. "I trust you've all gone over these lists of candidates, and the pictures Harvey dug up of each of them, so let's get down to business and eliminate the dogs right away."

Amidst much laughter and the sort of comments usually reserved for cattle buyers at an auction, the photos were passed around and the list quickly whittled down to fifteen men. Twice Sarah had to bite her tongue to keep from casually adding Brad's name to the growing list of rejects, hoping in vain someone else would do it for her.

Chucking the losers' photos back into the folder, Miriam spread the rest out on the table in front of her. "Well, that's progress, but five of these have still got to go. Let's get brutal."

Harvey pushed away from the table, laughing. "I abstain from here on in. Why can't we do a feature on the ten sexiest women in the city instead?"

Predictably, Miriam was instantly intrigued. "That's something to think about. Sarah, let's make a note to discuss that later."

Sarah nodded grimly, wishing Harvey's shins were in kicking distance under the table. "Let's get this one tucked away first, shall we?" She moved the photos of Lance Carter and an actor with the local repertory theatre away from the rest. "I think we can all agree that these two are definites."

"And these," chimed in Kelly Hargraves, an editorial assistant, adding the photos of a college professor and a concert promoter to the pile. Three more men quickly joined the list of "winners"—none of them Brad—and Sarah felt a glimmer of hope. Her palms turned damp as Miriam filled the eighth slot with a local gynecologist to unanimous approval, and then silence reigned.

It seemed incredible to Sarah that Brad was languishing in a group that inspired no clear-cut feeling one way or the other in her co-workers. Irrationally, her desperate hope that he be passed over was turning into resentment that he might possibly be rejected in favor of a bunch of men who obviously couldn't hold a candle to him in looks or personality or even accomplishments, for that matter.

Miriam pushed her glasses back on her nose and tapped her pen decisively. "All right, I say the piano teacher, Bartholomew what's-his-name, goes. Just that name is reason enough." There was a general murmur of agreement. "And the judge."

A short silence followed, in which Sarah couldn't believe she heard herself say, in an offhand tone that in no way reflected the emotions churning within, "Oh, I don't know, Miriam. Brad Chandler seems like a good prospect to me. Certainly better than, say, Jiggs, that hairy concert promoter."

"Oh, no." Sally's blond head shook firmly. "Chandler's not bad, but he doesn't compare to Jiggs. He just hasn't got what we're looking for. I vote no."

"Well, I vote yes," Sarah shot back stubbornly.

"Let's try and look at this professionally," interceded Miriam. "Thinking in terms of the potential photographs for the article, I have to agree with Sally that Jiggs fits in with the image we're trying to convey better than somebody swathed in black robes."

It was the perfect out, and in her head Sarah knew it. But in her heart she felt a compulsion to defend Brad to the bitter end. "Maybe, but Brad Chandler is involved in areas much more interesting than his career as a judge, and much more interesting than hordes of screaming teenagers. For instance, he designs and builds his own sailboats."

"Is he affiliated with any of the Cup contenders?" asked Miriam, and Sarah could sense the level of interest in the small room rising.

"No," she admitted, watching the interest evaporate

into thin air. "But he's considering turning it into a full-time career someday."

Sally rolled her eyes. "Fascinating."

"It could be," said Kelly, jumping into the fray. "And he is gorgeous. Look at this picture of him smiling. I love the way those dimples slash across his cheeks. That's sexy."

Brenda, a staff reporter, picked up the picture in question and squinted at it. "I don't know. Doesn't he look sort of short?"

"It's the camera angle," Sarah rushed to explain, striving for nonchalance, knowing she sounded defensive instead. "And that dark jacket. Take a look at this one."

Brenda obligingly examined the picture of Brad standing on the courthouse steps, his tie loosened, jacket slung over his shoulder, one hip casually angled in what Sarah considered a very sexy manner. "I guess so," Brenda finally said. "Too bad we don't have a picture of him in a bathing suit, like that lifeguard."

"Brenda," Kelly admonished, chuckling. "This isn't exactly the Mr. America pageant."

Brenda shrugged. "What can I say? I'm a leg-woman at heart. Actually, all seven of the leftovers look about equal to me."

Leftovers. Sarah bit her lip. What had ever made her think this crew was the least bit astute?

"Except for that eye-in-the-sky weatherman." Kelly wrinkled her nose. "His mustache droops on one side."

Miriam scooped up and disposed of the weatherman's photos. "It's down to these six, and we only need two. Shall we make it a secret ballot in the interest of office harmony?" She looked from Sarah to Sally.

"Not on my account." Sally shrugged. "As long as the article is a success, I don't really care who's in it."

"Me, either," lied Sarah. "Let's just get it over with. I have tons of work to finish before I leave here tonight."

It was over in a matter of minutes, with a quick show of hands, and when Sarah was handed the names and photos of the ten men selected, Brad's was not included—to her enormous relief. Sometime during the voting she'd come to her senses and realized what she'd almost done, and how little Brad would thank her for her efforts on his behalf. Her emotionally based defense of him was extremely out of character—as out of character as everything else she'd done that day—and it gave rise to some unsettling suspicions. It had been a purely gut reaction, the same sort of reaction she'd feel if someone had maligned her mother or her sister or . . . anyone else she loved, Sarah realized in a flash of intuition that stopped her dead in the act of gathering her papers together. This new wrinkle was much more than merely unsettling, and she felt an instinctive urge to retreat and gather her defenses.

"Sarah, I hope we didn't step on your toes with that last vote."

Sarah looked up in surprise. She'd thought everyone else had left the meeting together, but Miriam had obviously hung back to speak with her alone. "Not at all," she said emphatically. Then, with a chuckle, she added, "In fact, you all probably did me a favor."

Miriam grinned. "I take that to mean Brad isn't smitten with the prospect of being included in the article?"

"That's putting it mildly." She slanted a meaningful glance at her boss. "And I can't say I blame him. I mean how would you feel if this *were* an article on women and you were included?"

"Honey, at my age I'd sell my soul just to be a runner-up."

Sarah laughed at her boss's wistful expression. At fifty, Miriam Blakely was still a very attractive woman—tall, slender, with silver-blond hair and impeccable taste. "And you know, Miriam, I wouldn't swallow my gum in surprise if you were."

"Being publisher does give me some privileges around here," Miriam returned as they headed for the stairs together. "Like being able to tell you to get out of here on time tonight. Whatever's on your desk won't run away over the weekend."

"Maybe not, but it does seem to have the nasty habit of reproducing whenever my back is turned. Besides, I don't have any other plans." It was true. The long kiss she'd shared with Brad when he dropped her off at the office had promised much, but he'd opened the door for her with nothing more than a smiling, "I'll see you later."

They reached the second floor, where Sarah's office was, and Miriam paused to glance over Sarah's shoulder with lifted eyebrows and a very smug expression. "No plans, eh? If I were you I wouldn't bet next week's paycheck on that."

Sarah followed her gaze to where Brad sat reading a magazine outside her office. "I didn't know he was coming," she explained, drinking in the sight of him—the snug denims molding his long legs, the contrast of his bronzed forearms with the rolled-up sleeves of the white shirt, the soft darkness of his hair.

"For such a smart girl, Sarah, you can be pretty obtuse." Sarah swung around to see Miriam's head shaking slowly back and forth, a very transparent grin on her face. "I couldn't help noticing that the gentleman now parked outside your office is the same gentleman who picked you up last night *and* dropped you off—three hours late—this morning." She overrode Sarah's blushing effort to explain. "Coincidentally, he's also the same man who just inspired the only slip from cold, hard rationality I've witnessed from you in five years. And if all that adds up to what my years of experience tell me it does, all I can say is, it's about time. Now get out of here—that's an order."

This last was called over her shoulder as she continued down the stairs, leaving Sarah with a slowly fading blush on her face and a maelstrom of conflicting thoughts and desires raging within. She started walking slowly toward Brad, need battling want, her ingrained dedication to duty battling a brand new impulse to throw caution—and everything else that wasn't Brad—to the winds. Overlaying it all was an uneasy suspicion about the feelings that had motivated her behavior during the meeting, a suspicion that refused to bow to the inner voice coaching her to let tomorrow take care of itself.

At the sight of her Brad grinned and sprang to his feet, and Sarah felt her heartbeat quicken like one of Pavlov's dogs.

"This is a surprise." Somehow she managed a controlled tone and smile.

One dark brow lifted as he swept closer to brush her lips with his. "I don't see why it should be."

"You didn't mention anything about picking me up when you dropped me off this morning." There was an edge to her voice that she couldn't explain. She walked into her office, dropping some papers onto Melanie's deserted desk on the way. At this time on a Friday afternoon the only ones left in the building were probably the elderly janitor and her . . . and Brad.

"I just assumed you'd assume I'd be picking you up. You don't have your car," he pointed out.

Sarah shrugged. "I've walked before. And probably will tonight. I have hours of work to catch up on here."

Something hard crept into Brad's expression, tightening his square jaw. "That's out of the question."

"My working late?" She eyed him challengingly.

"I meant your walking home from here after dark. But as long as you brought it up, I don't see why the hell you have to work late on a Friday night. There's not another soul left in this place."

"That means fewer distractions. And among other things, the reason I have to work late is to make up for the time I lost this morning."

Warm hands cupped her shoulders from behind as she pretended to scan the afternoon mail. "Do you want to tell me about it?"

"About what?"

"About whatever happened between the time we 'lost' together this morning and now to make you start doubting what's between us."

"I don't even know what's between us yet," she said, sounding offhand but feeling like ice beneath the warmth of his fingers.

"Then let me tell you." His tone and the hands that turned her to face him were gentle, but there was a fire burning in his eyes very much like the one she'd seen there the night before. "It's really very simple. You belong to me, Sarah."

Her laugh sounded shaky, nervous. "This isn't the age of slavery, Brad. People don't belong to each other."

"Sure they do," he countered with stark certainty. "Except this type of possession can't be accomplished by the signing of a deed."

"Or by one night in bed."

"Is that what you think?" he demanded. "That I'm staking my claim on the basis of one night in bed with you?"

"Aren't you?" She searched his smoldering gaze for truths she was afraid to find . . . and almost more afraid not to.

"Not by a long shot. I told you before, my feelings for you have nothing to do with the number of days we've known each other." He cupped her chin, his thumb reaching up to stroke her bottom lip, slipping inside to trace the even line of her teeth in a gesture that was extraordinarily intimate.

"What *do* they have to do with?" she asked softly.

Smoky green eyes caressed her face. They were the eyes of a man reckless enough to walk away from the safe comfort of a promising career to chase after a dream, and strong enough to put the dream aside if that's what his conscience deemed right. No matter what his answer to her question, Sarah knew it would be no well-turned line. It would be the truth.

"It has to do with things you're not ready to hear," he said finally, his soft sigh mingling with her unsteady breathing. "It's a good thing I have the patience of a saint."

His mouth closed over hers in a very unsaintly manner. His tongue was a flame, sweeping past her lips, scorching, consuming, in a kiss that echoed his claim of possession more eloquently than words. Melting against him, Sarah moved with unconscious sensuousness, eliciting a soft laugh and a tightening of his embrace. He leaned into her, trapping her between the desk and the hard length of his body, then lifted his head, punctuating his hoarse words with licks at the corners of her mouth.

"Are you sure you have to work tonight?"

Sarah wasn't quite sure of anything, but she nodded dazedly. "I'm sure."

"But not tomorrow." It wasn't a question. "I want you with me tomorrow. I have a surprise for you. And on Sunday I'd like to take you to the welcoming party for the crew of the Australian Cup challenger."

She laughed up at him. "This weekend I'm yours."

A light danced in the eyes that pinned hers. "And I'm yours." He kissed her again, gently this time, and let her go. "Will you promise me you'll take a cab home, or do I have to park outside until you come out?"

She sighed resignedly, secretly thrilled by his concern. "I'll take a cab home."

He held her hand all the way to the office door, his thumb circling her palm with strokes she felt up and down her arm. "Don't forget."

"I won't forget."

"I know you won't, my sweet lady." Strong, slightly

rough fingers caged her face for a final kiss. "I won't let you."

The smoldering warning in his narrowed eyes told Sarah he was talking about much more than a cab ride. The feeling was confirmed later when a grinning delivery man, bribed by Brad into working overtime, showed up at her office door. He steadfastly refused the tip she offered, declaring it had all been taken care of, and smirked his way back out, leaving Sarah smiling at a dozen shiny red helium-filled balloons and a card that read, "From one of the ten sexiest men in town, to the sexiest lady he knows."

Chapter Six

SARAH AWOKE THE next morning to the sound of the telephone ringing and the sight of golden sunbeams dancing on the balloons tied to the foot of her bed.

Propping the receiver between her ear and the pillow, she managed a groggy "Hello," then smiled and stretched like a thoroughly stroked kitten as Brad's deep voice asked, "Did I wake you?"

"Mmm hmm. Good morning."

"It would be a hell of a lot better one if I were there with you."

His velvet growl elicited a shiver of heat and hunger that startled Sarah. Gripping the phone, she gave a shaky laugh. "If you were here, you'd be drowning in red balloons."

"If I were there, I'd be drowning in something a lot softer and sweeter than balloons." Sarah's breath caught at the raw intimacy in his hushed tone, and he chuckled softly into her silence. "But I'm glad to hear you dragged them home with you. I was afraid you were so angry with me last night you'd chuck them in the nearest dumpster."

"I wasn't angry," she countered, "just a little frightened by how quickly things seem to be going."

"Sometimes things go that way," he said softly, with a calm assurance that was catching. "But I probably don't help matters any by rushing you even more. Like now, for example," he added with a chuckle. "Can you be dressed and ready to go in thirty minutes?"

She sat up straight in the bed. "Not without the help of a hairdresser and a lady's maid."

"If I didn't have a stop to make on the way over, I'd volunteer, eagerly." His teasing grin transmitted clearly even over telephone wires. "Do the best you can, and when I get there I'll just sit around and watch you finish. On second thought, why don't you stay right where you are and—"

"I'll be ready in thirty minutes," Sarah interrupted, laughing.

When they hung up she was still smiling at his playfully disappointed sigh and glowing with excitement at the yearning evident in his provocative teasing. There was something thrilling about being wanted by a man like Brad, especially when her desire was a fiery echo of his own. In the clear morning light of a spring day that promised to be perfect, it was easy to push aside the misgivings that had shared her bed the night before.

She showered, fluffed her hair with a curling iron, and pulled on the casual clothes Brad had suggested, with one eye on the clock. When the doorbell rang thirty-five minutes after they'd said good-bye, she was just tucking a cream-colored cotton sweater into her jeans. She quickly added a narrow leather belt, a light spray of cologne, and—fumbling with a pair of tiny gold ball earrings—headed for the door. Lost in Brad's dazzling smile, at first she didn't notice the small boy on whose shoulders Brad's big hands rested.

"Sarah," he said, his smile overlaid with pride, "This is Tommy, my little brother. Do you mind if Tommy calls you Sarah?"

"No . . . of course not." She looked from Tommy back to Brad, trying to come to terms with both the obviously vast difference in their ages and Brad's claim on their "blind date" that he was an only child. "Your brother?" she said.

Brad smiled and winked. "That's right, through the Big Brother program. Neither one of us has any other brothers, so this is sort of special."

Sarah smiled down at the small, blond-haired boy eyeing her so suspiciously. "I'd say that makes it very special. I'm pleased to meet you, Tommy. You look like you're all set for a big game." She nodded at the white baseball uniform proclaiming him a member of the team sponsored by Driscoll Pharmacy.

Her show of interest perked him up a bit. "Yeah. We're playing East Bay Oil at ten. We don't usually take women to the game with us," he informed her, saying *women* with as much affection as most people say *lice*. "But Brad says you're all right."

"How gallant of him." Sarah let her smile travel up to the man towering above him. "Tommy, there's a jar of raisins on the kitchen counter. I'll bet you could use some extra energy for the game."

"Yeah, neat." The youngster flashed her an honest-to-goodness smile as he swept past in the direction Sarah indicated.

Alone with Brad, she folded her arms and narrowed her eyes. "So, I'm all right, am I?"

He immediately unfolded her arms, guiding them around his neck, and bent to nibble a path from her collarbone to her ear. "I think what I actually said was that you're breathtakingly beautiful and sexy as hell, but you know kids; they never listen."

His warm lips trailed across her cheek to cover her waiting lips in a kiss Sarah knew was intended to be quick and light. Someday quick, light kisses might be possible for them, but right now the splendor was still too new, and their lips clung helplessly until Tommy's voice, sounding very close and very disgusted, shattered the sweetness.

"We're going to be late, y'know."

Brad lifted his head slowly and sighed. "Tommy, did it ever occur to you there might be something in life more important than baseball?"

"Sure. Football," he replied instantly. "But the season doesn't start until September. Can we go now?"

The field where the Driscolls were to play East Bay Oil was on the other side of the city. Tommy was out of the car almost before it stopped, running to join his teammates already warming up on the field.

Reaching for Sarah's hand as they crossed to the low bleachers stretching along the chain-link fence, Brad greeted enough of the other spectators by name to convince Sarah he was no stranger to Saturday morning Little League games. With one long stride he vaulted to the top bench, then leaned down to grasp Sarah's hands, hauling her up beside him with effortless grace. He sat close, the soft faded denim of his pants rubbing against the darker, crisper fabric of hers, titillating the flesh beneath.

"Unless my powers of observation are slipping," he ventured, "I'd say you're less than thrilled with my little surprise."

Sarah shook her head, "Not at all. Just properly surprised. You never mentioned that you're a Big Brother."

"I guess I should have filled you in about that, and the game, beforehand," he admitted sheepishly. "But to tell you the truth, I was a little afraid you'd shoot the idea down. Tommy's a very important part of my life, and I wanted you to meet him."

The simple remark delivered in his eager tone hit Sarah where she was most vulnerable. Swallowing the lump in her throat, she kept her eyes glued to the action on the field. "Tommy seems like a very nice little boy."

"He's great; a normal, well-adjusted kid, thank God." Something in his voice drew Sarah's hand to cover his. Brad slanted her a grateful smile at the touch, then let his gaze slide back to the spot where Tommy was practicing swinging a bat almost as big as he was. "His normality is a miracle, considering all he's been through. It's also a credit to his mother. Nancy is terrific—smart, loving. Her only mistake was falling for an animal like Tommy's father."

Sarah waited a moment, then asked, "Is he dead?"

Brad's laugh was harsh. "No such luck; just missing. Not that his absence is any great loss. He never worked— just hung out and drank and slapped around Tommy and his mother."

"Oh, Brad, that's awful!" Sarah exclaimed.

"The last time it happened was three years ago, when Nancy was pregnant with the twins. Fortunately she had the good sense to grab Tommy and get out. With the help of the women's shelter here in the city, she got a restraining order against the creep and filed for divorce. The thought of paying alimony and child support must have been more than he could take, because he bolted, and they haven't seen him since." There was an underlying tension in his short laugh and in every line of his tautly held body. "If he's smart, he'll keep it that way."

"Couldn't you take legal action forcing him to pay if he showed up?"

"You can't get blood from a stone," he said roughly. "Besides, if I ever got my hands on him, I wouldn't have the patience to take a legal approach." Barely controlled fury colored his voice, confirming Sarah's mounting suspicion that Brad's involvement with Tommy and his family went way beyond a ball game and an occasional trek to the zoo. She felt proud and jealous and guilty all at once.

"I've thought about it a lot," he continued tersely, "and I just don't understand how a man—any man—

could get his kicks beating up on a woman that way, let alone his own four-year-old son." She could feel the shudder that passed through his body. "What an example for a kid that age."

Sarah slid her hand into his and squeezed it. "I'm sure your affection has more than countered any damage done. He's lucky to have you."

"That's what most people think. The truth is we're lucky to have each other. My own childhood wasn't so memorable, and Tommy gives me a chance to make up for it a little." As if sensing the concern behind the questioning look she shot him, Brad smiled and closed his fingers over hers snugly. "It was nothing like Tommy's, and nothing to be bitter about. My folks did their best, with the time they had to spare, but as for a sense of closeness with my father, it just wasn't there." His eyes warmed as they traced the movements of the small, blond boy on the field. "It's there between Tommy and me, and I'll make damn sure it's there with my own children someday."

The soft oath struck Sarah like a blow in the stomach, leaving her with a faint nausea that felt as though it would never go away.

Brad's eyes narrowed at the sight of her stricken expression. "I hope that sad look isn't in honor of my forlorn childhood. I never doubted my parents' love, Sarah, and I had everything most kids only dream of."

She forced a smile. "Poor little rich boy?"

"Something like that." He grinned. "But if I do say so myself, I didn't turn out half bad."

"I don't know if I'd go that far," Sarah drawled, eyeing him with a critical squint.

He squeezed her hand harder. "Careful, love, it's a long walk home."

His casual use of the word *love* did strange things to her pulse rate, and she ran her eyes over him again for the sheer pleasure of it. "Now that I take a second look,

I'm forced to concur. You're not half bad."

"Smart lady." Lifting her hand to his lips, he kissed her palm, then circled the spot slowly with his tongue. Excitement rippled through Sarah's body like lightning. Brad's mouth curved in a pleased smile. "I'm going to have to remember how much you like that . . . for some time when we're not in the middle of a crowd."

The umpire shouted "Play ball," and a cheer went up from the small crowd as the two teams hustled into position. East Bay Oil batted first, getting off to an early lead that changed hands almost every inning. Brad joined in with the fathers of Tommy's teammates, shouting advice and encouragement from the sidelines, rivaling any of them for pride whenever their team made what he termed a "nice play." When Tommy made a wild slide for home plate in the last inning to score the winning run, Brad dragged Sarah from the seat with him in a rocking, bone-crushing hug.

"Did you see that kid fly? Isn't he something?"

Sarah was glad the questions were rhetorical and thankful for the parents swarming around Brad, slapping him on the back in an overflow of praise for the youngster they knew was his reason for being there. It gave her at least an illusion of privacy, a chance to take a deep breath and conjure up a smile. Inside, all she felt were steadily tightening wires of tension, a relentless grinding of nerves that escalated with each thrilled word, each look of unrestrained pride, from Brad. The sight of Tommy detouring by the fence on his way back to the dugout, his tiny face erupting in an ear-to-ear grin at a simple thumbsup sign from the man at her side, only added to her misery. But it wasn't Tommy's place in Brad's life that worried her; it was her own. Could there even *be* a place for a woman like her in the life of a man with Brad's yearning for a family of his own?

Ironically, that question brought the answer to the one that had haunted her since yesterday's editorial meeting.

In utter defiance of her own best interests—and of the pages on the calendar—she had gone ahead and fallen in love with Brad Chandler. Watching him now, she realized she loved him in a way that bounced everything else in her life into second place and made her want to give him the sun and the stars—everything. That she would never be able to give him the one thing that might matter most was the cloud around the silver lining of loving him.

Feeling like Scarlett O'Hara, Sarah tried to thrust aside the spectre of the future until later, tomorrow, sometime when she could be alone to sort out the pieces of a puzzle that might never fit together. It was a challenge, especially when Brad announced that their Saturday ritual included picking up Tommy's mother and twin sisters for a trip to a local pizza place.

To her surprise, Sarah hit it off with Nancy—a pretty, slightly plump blonde around her own age—from the second she climbed into the car, leaned over the seat to check Sarah out, then fell back with an anguished, "Thin! Why is everyone in the world except me thin?"

Brad chuckled as he slid behind the wheel. "It's called willpower, Nancy, and you don't have any."

"I'll have you know that since the twins were born I've lost seven hundred pounds," she informed him haughtily. "Unfortunately, it happens to be the same fifteen pounds, over and over and over..." She trailed off, only to lean forward and poke him in the shoulder with renewed vengeance. "Besides, who are you to talk to me about willpower? I'm not the one who's invested a fortune in video arcades, one quarter at a time."

"Quiet, woman," ordered Brad, laughing at her in the rearview mirror. "I'm trying to impress Sarah with my maturity and sophistication."

Nancy snorted. "And I'm going to star in a diet cola commercial."

The bantering continued during the short drive to

Cappy's—a restaurant boasting great pizza, old car-
toons, and rows of video games—setting the tone for
the afternoon.

Nancy was fun to be with, and she handled the kids—
and Brad—with the humorous efficiency of an affec-
tionate drill sergeant, keeping the inevitable confusion
involved in dining with three noisy little kids and an
indulgent big one to a tolerable level. Despite the unavoidable references to previous outings and the easy flow
of inside jokes, both Brad and Nancy went out of their
way to make Sarah feel included. And she did. Only in
the very back of her mind did the notion hover that this
felt like a perfect family outing—Mom, Dad, the
kids . . . and a friendly, old-maid aunt.

They attacked the two large cheese-and-pepperoni
pizzas with gusto, and in record time all that remained
was a single piece. Sarah, who'd surrendered after her
third slice, had to laugh at Brad and Nancy, who were
both eyeing it longingly.

"C'mon, let's split it," Brad finally grumbled with a
pretense of exasperation.

"I couldn't," insisted Nancy, her palm already outstretched for her half.

Brad went along with what was obviously a well-worn
joke, thrusting the torn pizza at her with a firm, "I insist.
You can start your diet tomorrow."

"Well, as long as you insist." They bit into their pizza
at the same time, both chuckling. As soon as Nancy had
swallowed the last bite she stared at her plate and shook
her head miserably. "Why did I eat that last piece? It
must be nerves, motherhood . . . the pressure, the monotony. I used to be a size seven back B.C.," she told
Sarah.

"Before children," Brad explained laughingly. Then,
reaching over to squeeze Nancy's shoulder in an affec-
tionate gesture that Sarah noted with mixed emotions,

he said, "Cheer up, Nance. You've got something a lot more valuable than a sleek figure. Would you honestly trade the kids to be a size seven again?"

"Ask me again when I'm trapped with them on a rainy day," she retorted, wiping tomato sauce from Amanda's jersey and deftly adjusting the ribbon on Rebecca's braid.

"Speaking of trapped," Brad said, green eyes dancing at Tommy and the little girls who were already giggling in anticipation, "I suppose you guys are going to con me into playing Donkey-Kong again?"

The youngsters responded with enthusiastically affirmative shouts, tumbling from the big booth. Under cover of the table, Brad's hand swept like wildfire along the length of Sarah's thigh as he slid out to join them. He turned back with a crooked grin. "Can you ladies find something to talk about while we're gone?"

"Sure. You," Nancy shot back.

The rhythm of his laugh was alluring, and Sarah found herself wishing he wouldn't leave, not even for a few minutes.

"I'm flattered," he said in response to Nancy's flip remark.

"Don't be so hasty," she cautioned, smiling sweetly. Then, to Brad's amusement and the horror of the elderly couple across the aisle, she called after him. "And don't blow all the grocery money on those damn games again this week."

The two women stared into their sodas, trying not to laugh, not daring to make eye contact until the shocked old gentleman and his wife turned back to their plates of spaghetti.

"I have got to stop doing that to him," Nancy vowed solemnly. "Bad enough maligning a judge in public, but if he does become a U.S. senator..." She trailed off, shaking her head at the thought.

"A senator?"

Nancy stared at Sarah, obviously taken aback by her
widened eyes and surprise-riddled question. "Hasn't Brad
told you?"

Sarah shrugged with a casualness she was far from
feeling. "I guess not. What's this about his becoming a
U.S. senator?"

The other woman sipped her soda, apparently trying
to decide how much, if anything, she should divulge. "I
don't know that much about it myself," she said finally.
"Only that Brad's been asked to consider running for
John Coswell's seat when Coswell retires next year.
Needless to say, he's less than thrilled by the prospect
of all that pomp and circumstance." She rolled her eyes,
laughing. "You know Brad."

Do I? wondered Sarah, smiling back. She took a long
sip of her soda while she gathered her thoughts. Until a
few hours ago she thought she knew Brad with a fullness
that was a miracle after such a short time. So much for
miracles. Glancing up, she found Nancy watching her
with a very worried expression.

"Look," she said earnestly, "I sure hope I haven't said
something I shouldn't have. If I've caused trouble between you and Brad, he'll wring my neck."

"Your neck is safe," Sarah forced herself to assure
Nancy. "Brad probably just hasn't gotten around to men-
tioning it. We haven't known each other that long, and
I'm sure we're both in for a lot of surprises as we get
better acquainted."

Nancy's sigh of relief was audible. "This seems to be
a day for surprises. I felt that way myself when Brad
mentioned he was bringing you to the game."

"I hope you didn't mind?"

"Oh, no," Nancy replied instantly. Then she formed
a slightly sheepish grin. "But you just stole my line. I
hope *you* don't mind us." She waved a hand around the
empty booth as if her family were still there. "I mean,

all the time Brad spends with Tommy and the rest of us."

Reading the mixture of concern and hope etched in the other woman's eyes, Sarah thought about all Nancy had been through, and her heart went out to her. "Never. I think it's wonderful. In Brad's words, Tommy and he are lucky to have each other."

Nancy smiled slightly and nodded. "Yes, that's something Brad would say. He's been a lifesaver. Sometimes I feel he's as much a big brother to me as to Tommy."

There was a wistful catch in her voice that stirred a possessive instinct Sarah knew she had no right to feel. She intentionally forced the conversation on to lighter topics, asking Nancy about her work as a practical nurse, describing her current problem article, and swearing Nancy to silence about Brad's being omitted until she had a chance to break it to him gently. She hadn't quite had the heart yet. True, he'd been opposed to the idea all along, but she had a sneaky suspicion that, as he'd jokingly said, being left out was going to be much more bruising to his ego than being included in the first place.

That was only one of the things on her mind as she continued to smile through the rest of the afternoon, forcing herself to join in the continual lighthearted bantering until they dropped Nancy and the kids off at their door. Once she was alone with Brad, the effort suddenly became too much, and she let her head roll back on the seat, eyes closed. She felt the touch of Brad's fingers on her cheek, hard and gentle and as warm as the slowly setting sun.

"You look exhausted." His deep voice was another kind of caress. "Kids will do that to you when you aren't used to being around them. We'll have to build up your endurance slowly."

She smiled without opening her eyes, beyond formulating some meaningless reply that wouldn't even scratch the surface of what she was really feeling. Her emotions were a maze of questions, doubts, and fears she had neither the energy nor the courage to tackle tonight. The day had left her with an intense desire for one thing only: to be held in the arms of the man she loved. She was happy when Brad followed her into her apartment without hesitation, as if they'd come home together hundreds of times before.

It felt like that again when he pulled her into his arms behind the closed door, their bodies melting against each other as if hundreds of embraces had shaped and molded the heat and steel of his flesh into a perfect complement for her soft curves. He held her tightly against him, kissing her as though she were water and he was dying of thirst. His mouth coaxed and demanded at once, relearning her textures with a slow moving tongue.

Sarah returned his kiss with a hunger born of desperation, parting her lips at his first velvet thrust, offering him all that was hers to give. She felt the muscles of his back twist and ripple beneath her fingers as he obeyed her silent command to angle closer, their kiss deepening steadily, furiously, until she heard a small sound from deep in her throat and felt Brad pull away.

His breath brushed her ear in a heated rush. "Whoa, slow down, love. Tell me what's the matter."

Her defensiveness sprang between them like a shield of ice.

"Nothing is the matter." She tried to shrug from his embrace and, after an assessing perusal of her face, Brad complied. "If you don't want to kiss me," she added, turning away, "just say so."

Gripping her arm, he spun her back to face him before she'd taken half a step. "What the hell are you talking about? You know I want to kiss you. In fact, I want to do a whole lot more than kiss you. I'd like to take you down on this floor with me right now and make love to you until you scream with pleasure."

She swallowed hard and stared straight into green eyes that were narrowed, smoky with concern. "Then do it."

"I will." The husky promise flowed over her like raw silk. "I need that, and I know you do, too. But first I need to know what's bothering you. And don't lie and tell me it's nothing. I can feel it in your body when I hold you. Even in your kiss." He dragged his fingers through the midnight satin of his hair. "Does it have something to do with today?"

Sarah sighed and stared at a point somewhere over his shoulder. His eyes, his voice, every line of his body told her he was ready to hear what she wasn't ready to tell. She gave a small shrug and took the easy way out. "I guess I just didn't like finding out you might soon be Senator Chandler from someone else."

He stared at her incredulously, started to smile, then shook his head. "Is that what this is all about?"

"You could have told me."

"I would have, if it were half as important as you seem to think it is. It has nothing to do with us."

"Does it have to do with Nancy?"

"Are you jealous?"

"Of course not."

He stared at her a moment, weighing that response. Then, much more softly, he said, "I didn't tell you the first night because I just didn't think of it. It's not on my mind twenty-four hours a day. Then, once you told me about the article, I didn't tell you because I was afraid you'd think I was using it to pressure you into changing your mind. What you have planned isn't exactly a politician's dream of favorable publicity," he explained dryly.

With the realization that he'd kept it from her to make her life easier, love for him came in a wave so intense she ached. "I wouldn't be so sure about that," Sarah whispered, moving back into arms that opened eagerly at her approach. "I think you'd win the female vote hands down."

"There's only one female whose vote interests me." His hands were busy freeing the cotton sweater from her jeans. Sarah leaned a bit to simplify his task and was rewarded by the warmth of his hands on the skin over her ribs.

"It's a relief to know you're interested in me for my mind," she breathed against the side of his neck before succumbing to the urge to taste the heated, male-scented flesh there. He trembled as her tongue made contact.

"Oh, I am, I am. Haven't you ever heard that the mind is the most erogenous zone of the whole human body?"

"Mmm. I've always wondered if it's true."

"We're about to find out."

With a marvelously magical movement, he lowered them both to the floor, bringing her down on the cushion of his body. Lying back, he let his arms fall open and closed his eyes, issuing a silent invitation Sarah couldn't resist. She flowed over him freely, touching him through his clothes with ardent lips and fingers, enjoying his involuntary trembling, the way his breathing quickened.

Straddling his hips, she dragged up first his shirt, then her own, and leaned closer until her soft breasts met the tantalizingly rough hair that curled across his chest. Brad twisted beneath her with a hoarse groan of pleasure and, locking his hands behind her neck, pulled her mouth down to his.

Here, too, though, he let her take the lead, waiting patiently while her lips brushed his eyelids and the high bones of his cheeks before her own clamoring desire drove her to claim his mouth in a kiss that was hungry, penetrating. His response to that was anything but passive. His rough-velvet tongue parted her lips fully, plunging into the dampness of her mouth with a fevered blend of skill and passion until Sarah was as much seduced as seductress.

She felt hot and cold at once, her body alive with a

primitive need and the thrilling anticipation of having it satisfied. Neither of them said a word, relying on a vocabulary of strokes and touches that was as old as man and woman. Their hands wove mysterious patterns of sensation, coaxing, commanding, discovering each other's secret areas of pleasure and elevating them to places of worship.

Sarah's contented sigh turned into a deep purr as Brad's thumb scoured her breast, rushing her senses with echos of delight. Like warm honey her fingers glided over his chest, hesitating a fraction of a second at the leather obstacle of his belt before sliding lower. Her touch was firm and sure, claiming his heat through the soft denim, and Brad arched against her with a furious thrust that reversed their positions and left her panting up at him.

"I thought *I* was running this show," she teased shakily, unconsciously matching the slow, rotating motion of his hips.

"I thought so, too, but I was wrong." He flashed her a crooked smile, revealing his dimples, but his hooded eyes and strained breathing spoke of a passion that was barely leashed. "I thought I'd be able to let you tease me to your heart's content." He swallowed hard. "I didn't know I could want a woman so badly I could come close to losing control."

Sarah held her breath, then whispered, "And?"

The twin fires blazing in his eyes moved closer by spellbinding degrees. "And now I know."

Chapter Seven

SUNDAY EVENING'S PARTY to welcome the Cup chal-
lengers from Australia was held at the Beechwood estate,
a properly grand setting for a gathering of Newport's
elite. The warm night air beckoned most of the partygoers
through the French doors to the patio that sprawled behind the pale yellow, stuccoed brick mansion. There,
hundreds of candles twinkling inside crystal globes and
flickering in towering wrought-iron holders cast a dream-
like glow over the elegant celebration.

In direct contrast to the romantic setting were the
lively antics of the Australian crew and their American
counterparts. Fueled by the freely flowing champagne,
they added a splash of rowdiness to the party that seemed
to dismay the formally attired bluebloods in attendance.
Most of them, anyway. It was painfully obvious from
the listless way Brad was nodding at whatever the short
man by his side was saying that he would much rather
loosen his black tie and join the insurgents who had
hijacked some of the band's instruments and were now
waging a vigorous duel of national anthems.

Watching him from across the patio, Sarah smiled with sympathy and a twinge of pride. Without a doubt he was the handsomest man in the place. His chiseled good looks and air of restless energy set him apart even in this sea of black tuxedoes. It seemed hard to believe that she was really here with him, that in a few minutes he would finish his business discussion and search her out again. A thrill that was equal parts memory and anticipation shot through her, and her smile deepened.

"It's not funny, Sarah."

At the hissing admonishment she turned to face Julie's annoyed glare. "I'm sorry, Julie. I wasn't laughing at what you said." Then, lifting her shoulders in an apologetic shrug, she asked, "What did you say?"

"I said," Julie bit out with obvious impatience, "that my dress and slip have developed a chemical incompatability. This damn slip has ridden up around my—"

"I get the picture," Sarah interrupted.

"Waist," finished Julie defiantly.

"You should use a fabric softener, or at least that anticling spray stuff," advised Sarah, darting a glance around to see if anyone else had noticed Julie's squirming.

"When I want hints from Heloise, I'll write to her. Just stand in front of me so I can fix it."

"Here?"

Julie rolled her eyes disgustedly. "Doesn't anything like this ever happen to you?"

"Yes, but I handle it in private."

"Well, by the time I walk to where it's private, my slip will be wrapped around my neck," Julie retorted, positioning herself between Sarah and a dense cluster of rose bushes.

Sarah scanned the gathering over the rim of her champagne glass, nervously aware of Julie's frantic activity behind her. Fortunately, everyone else seemed engrossed in the poolside escapades of several young sailors— everyone except the tall, dark-haired man with piercing green eyes watching her from across the patio. For a second he seemed genuinely puzzled by her rigid stance and self-conscious half wave; then his eyes crinkled above a broad smile, and Sarah saw him excuse himself from the group of men and start toward her at a quick pace.

"Hurry," she hissed over her shoulder. "Brad's headed this way."

"Good. Two bodies make a better screen than one. Besides, I'm sure he's seen——"

"Just hurry," Sarah repeated as Brad arrived at her side.

"Need a hand?" he asked in a voice tinged with humor.

"No thanks." Julie stepped from behind Sarah, the picture of propriety, her small handbag bulging with her rolled-up slip. "I know you two would love to have me stay and chat, but I *am* here on official station business." She glared at their joint snicker before gliding away with a cheery, "Have fun!"

"Is this supposed to be fun?" Brad asked her, his dark eyebrows lowering.

"You're the one who said you wanted to come."

"No, I said I wanted to bring you," he corrected firmly. "I *had* to come."

"Thanks a lot." Sarah poked him playfully in the ribs, getting a sweet thrill from even that slight contact. "So I'm here because misery loves company?"

There was no responding laughter in his compelling green eyes or his low-pitched voice. "No, because I love you."

Around them the party spun on crazily, a kaleidoscope of color and babble they neither saw nor heard as they were plummeted into another, intensely private dimension by three timeless little words. They might have stood there, their eyes clinging—hers surprised, faintly confused; his searching, begging for a deeper response—until the candles burned out and the musicians packed up to go home, if it hadn't been for the husky, gray-haired man who slapped Brad on the back with a boisterous, "There you are, old buddy."

Brad dragged his gaze from Sarah, obviously struggling to shift emotional gears, and greeted the intruder with a decided lack of enthusiasm. "Oh, Bob, nice to see you."

"And you." The man pumped Brad's hand vigorously. "And even nicer to see your friend here."

Unabashed pride shaded Brad's smile and sent warmth rippling through her. "Sarah, this is Bob Purini, chairman of the state Democratic party. Bob, I'd like you to meet Sarah Templeton." He added no explanatory tag. None was needed. His arm settling comfortably around her waist, riding her hip, said it all.

"I'm happy to meet you, Sarah."

Shaking the man's hand briefly, Sarah smiled and returned the sentiment. Brad had mentioned Bob Purini that afternoon when they'd discussed in detail the possibility of his running for the Senate, and she knew that most of the pressure involved came from this man. She also knew from the calculated way he was eyeing her from head to toe that she was being evaluated as a potential campaign asset.

"And may I say you look beautiful this evening?" he added.

She murmured a quick thank you. Despite the reason for his favorable assessment, Sarah liked hearing it. And she agreed with it. In fact, she was getting used to feeling beautiful, and she knew it had far less to do with the clingy, raspberry silk gown that left one shoulder provocatively bare than it did with the green-eyed man at her side.

After a few polite moments of general remarks, Purini adroitly steered the conversation to the issue of Brad's political future. Brad fielded both the leading questions and the blatant ego-strokes with a tongue-in-cheek carelessness that charmed Sarah and clearly frustrated the older man.

Freezing a small, interested smile in place as the two entered a jousting match about platform concessions and career priorities, Sarah anxiously mulled over the moment just before they were interrupted. It wasn't that thoughts of love and Brad existed separately in her own mind. Far from it. But hearing it said out loud, with such matter-of-fact certainty by a man she knew did not play coy little games, propelled it from the realm of fantasy into the harsh light of reality. And instead of being the promise of happily-ever-after that it ought to be, his love seemed like the shiny gold ring suspended just out of reach on the merry-go-round.

How could he love her when he didn't really know her? And he never would until she was honest about all that she was . . . and wasn't. In that instant of awareness Sarah felt a stab of concern for Brad and his feelings that was greater than any she could ever feel for herself. She had to tell him the truth, not before *she* fell so deeply in love that ending it would be heart-shattering, but before he did. Feeling a sense of desperation that clogged her windpipe, she became hazily aware that the conversation had shifted again, to something to do with her, and Brad was pointedly inviting her to join in.

"The magazine article," he prompted helpfully. "I told Bob you've graciously decided to include me in a feature in next month's issue." The pure deviltry in his eyes told Sarah that he may have mentioned the article, but the bombshell was hers to drop.

"Yes, well, it's not really about Brad," she hedged, remembering that he still didn't know he'd been eliminated and certain that this was not the moment to enlighten him.

"But I will be featured," Brad hastened to point out.

"That's great," Purini raved. "Every little bit of public exposure helps a candidate."

Brad's mouth twitched at the corners. "Oh, I'd say this definitely qualifies as public exposure, wouldn't you, Sarah?"

She gave a small nod and flashed him a warning look he completely ignored.

"I want to hear all about it," said Purini.

"Tell him all about it, Sarah," Brad echoed, obviously playing the scene sheerly for its shock value.

She hesitated, searching for a way to travel that thin line between truth and an out-and-out lie. "It's just an article about ten local residents."

Purini nodded, obviously calculating its potential value, while Brad stood by shaking his head almost imperceptibly, his eyes brimming with an amused challenge she couldn't resist.

"Ten men," she added.

Brad's laughing gaze never wavered.

"The ten sexiest men in Newport, to be precise." It came out in a slurred rush.

Bob Purini sprayed a mouthful of champagne back into his glass. "What did you say?"

"She said the ten sexiest men in Newport," Brad supplied helpfully.

"She can't do that to you." In his green-at-the-gills state Purini seemed not to notice Brad's outrageously pleased grin.

"She has to," Brad pointed out. "It's her job."

"The hell with her job! We're talking about your whole future."

"Relax, Bob. Think of the exposure I'll be getting. In fact, I heard they're planning a banquet to honor the chosen. Maybe you can arrange to have me speak."

"Speak?" Purini croaked. "You can't even go. Do you have any idea the kind of ammunition a thing like this will give your opponent? I can see the slogans now: Do You Want to Send a Playboy to Washington?"

Brad's poker-faced nod had Sarah biting the inside of

her cheek to keep from laughing. "That's very catchy. Maybe we should use it ourselves."

Purini stared at him as if he'd just grown horns and lowered his voice to a desperate plea. "Brad, we have to talk—"

"And we will," Brad broke in, "but I just saw Barry Ferguson over there and remembered I was supposed to get back to him about something before tomorrow. You know me and responsibility," he called back to the still-sputtering Purini, tugging Sarah with him across the crowded patio.

Her high heels clicked against the flagstones, then sank into the thick cushion of the lawn as they rounded the corner of the house, flying past a mystified Julie without a pause.

"Brad, what are you doing?" Sarah demanded as they left the lights and sounds of the party behind.

"Escaping," he shot back without breaking stride.

"But what about the fireworks?" She stopped dead in her tracks and hitched a thumb toward the barge floating a hundred yards out in the Rhode Island Sound. On it were the makings of what promised to be a very bright, very noisy finale to the party. "I've been waiting all night for them."

Brad swung around with a sigh and tipped her face up to his. "Sarah, if you leave with me now, I promise you'll see fireworks before the night is over. If we stay, I promise that Purini will harangue us until we're both too tired to do so much as light a sparkler."

Sarah's smile spread slowly. "Well, when you put it like that . . ."

He didn't wait for the rest. "I thought you'd see it my way. Now move it."

"I'm moving," she grumbled, running to keep pace with his long stride.

They skirted the front of the house—Brad lifted her over a low hedge to reach the front walk—then streaked past the bewildered valets hired to fetch the guests' cars. They didn't look back until they reached Brad's BMW. Safely inside, the laughter they'd fought earlier bubbled to the surface.

"His face!" Sarah gasped, tears rolling down her cheeks. "I'll never forget the look on his face. He actually spit that mouthful of champagne."

Brad threw his head back and roared. "We're lucky he didn't spit his teeth out he was so surprised. He's been hounding me for so long, it's almost worth being in that article just to give him a few more gray hairs."

"Telling him about the article was bad enough, but did you have to lie about going to the banquet? And offering to speak, no less!"

Brad's grin faded to a gentle curving of his lips as his eyes met hers. "I wasn't lying. I intend to go."

Sarah blinked in confusion. "But why? I thought you hated the idea of the article."

"I do." He reached out and brushed her cheek with the back of his fingers. "But I wouldn't let you down by not showing up." His index finger pressed against her lips as she started to speak. "And don't ask me why; I've already told you. I'll go to your damn banquet for the same reason I wanted you here with me tonight, the reason I want you with me every night, all night, the reason I'd try to walk on water if you asked me to—I love you, Sarah."

The words were just as overwhelming the second time around, only now the two of them were alone and it was Brad who interrupted their passion-gilded look by placing his lips ever so lightly against hers. Sarah closed her eyes and surrendered to the magic of his gentleness. It was a tender kiss of discovery and wonder that taught them that feather strokes and restrained caresses could excite them as much and leave them every bit as breathless as hungrier, more aggressive ones if the mood was right. Brad broke away with a violent tremor that mirrored her own and tilted his head back to smile at her.

"Fireworks," whispered Sarah.

Brad's dark head shook in a slow denial. "That was just the warmup. The best is yet to come."

The best is yet to come. Those words rattled around in Sarah's mind as they drove back to her house. She knew Brad was talking about much more than the passion they would share in the next few hours. He was talking about the future, probably making plans and dreaming dreams she would never be able to fulfill. By the time they'd settled comfortably on the glider on her back porch, the need to tell him the truth had become a fever, blotting all else from her mind.

She was grateful, if somewhat puzzled, when he chose to sit at the far end of the glider, guiding its gentle sway with a flexing motion of one long leg. She liked the insulation the few feet separating them allowed, and she wished she hadn't automatically turned on the small table lamp. It bathed the screened-in porch with a soft, golden glow that would expose every expression flickering across Brad's face . . . and her own.

"Is it because I said I love you?" Brad's deep voice was totally devoid of emotion, and Sarah had to play the line over in her head before she was convinced she'd heard it straight.

"I'm not sure what you mean."

His eyes caught hers. "The reason you're pulling away from me again—is it because I told you that I'm in love with you?" He raked his fingers through his hair, creating tousled midnight waves Sarah's fingers longed to smooth. "I know I should go slowly with you. I've known from the start that you're vulnerable. Too vulnerable."

Sarah gave a short, impatient laugh. "Julie and that stupid blind date."

"It has nothing to do with anything Julie told me. It has to do with . . ." He shrugged. "I guess body language is as good a term as any. Reading people is part of my job, Sarah, and everything about you screams that you'll bolt if I push too hard, too fast." His laugh was harsh, dying away much too quickly to be genuine. "But I've gone and done it anyway. I guess I'm not as adept at interpreting signals as I thought. I could have sworn you were feeling a little bit of what I'm feeling."

It was a question, a plea, and there was no way on earth Sarah could look into the green eyes that had become an integral part of her existence and leave it unanswered.

"I am, and not just a little bit." She hesitated and licked dry lips with an equally dry tongue. "If I'm quiet, it's not because of anything you said. It's because of something I have to say, something I have to tell you." Wanting to tell him didn't make the words come any easier, and Sarah was sure that if bodies did speak, hers was delivering a soliloquy on the many faces of panic.

Brad angled into the corner of the glider, hitching the leg that wasn't propelling them back and forth up onto the green-and-white batik cushion. "Sounds ominous. Would it make it any easier on you if I told you there is absolutely nothing you could say that would affect my love for you?"

His smile, his words, even his carefree posture seemed to offer a safety net Sarah wouldn't permit herself to believe in. Not yet, anyway.

"A very noble sentiment," she said in a voice that was straining to stay at a normal register, "and a premature one. I know Julie told you I had a bad experience with a man a while back, but I don't know how much she told you."

"Only what you just did, which is all I need to know."

"Not quite." She paused, arranging words, rearranging them. Her hands became perfectly still. "It happened while I was in graduate school. Rod—that was his name—was a teaching assistant for one of my journalism professors. He asked me out and—" She faltered, thinking, And what, Sarah? And because I was foolish and insecure enough to let a man I could never love sweep me off my feet, I'll probably lose the man I do.

His soft, deep whisper filled the silence. "You don't have to tell me this, Sarah. In fact, it must be an intrinsically masculine flaw in my character that I don't want to hear all about the man who had you before I did. Sarah, I feel as though my life began again when I met you. Let it be that way for you, too."

"If only it could." She drew an anguished breath. "You're right; you don't have to hear all the boring details, but you do have to know this much. I want you to to know. My affair"—her lips twisted over the word—"with Rod lasted for the grand total of two weeks before he dumped me—something about me being lacking in every way he could imagine, and a few he couldn't."

Brad reached out and massaged her shoulder tenderly. It was almost more comforting than Sarah could bear, and she stiffened against the cushions. "The world is full of foolish men, Sarah," he said quietly. "You just happened to be unlucky enough to latch on to one at a young age."

She laughed bitterly, still not facing him but feeling his eyes on her like a caress. "I was a whole lot unluckier than that. After we broke up, I found out I was pregnant." She felt Brad's startled reaction through his fingertips on her shoulder, and she finished the story like a record on the wrong speed. "I had a miscarriage. The doctors called it a complicated miscarriage and told me I would never be able to have children."

She didn't know what reaction she expected from him. Not immediate rejection: Brad was too kind for that. If this revelation ended their relationship, it would be because it closed doors on their future together, not because it turned him against her for something that had happened years ago, something she couldn't have controlled. His fingers shifted to rest on the cushion behind her, breaking their only point of physical contact, and when Sarah couldn't stand the agony of not knowing what he was feeling for one second longer she forced her eyes to meet his.

"Why are you telling me this?" he asked, his voice the most neutral sound she'd ever heard, and the most frightening.

It was the one reaction she hadn't anticipated: no reaction at all. And that question. Lord, why *had* she told him? Because he'd lightly said "I love you" after a few glasses of champagne at a party? As soon as the humiliating possibility occurred to her, Sarah's common sense overrode it. That wasn't how he'd said it, or why. Whatever was prompting Brad's distance now, he'd meant those words.

Drawing courage from that, she searched his face more closely for answers and realized she wasn't going to find any. She realized the only reason she'd been able to read his moods so clearly up until now was because he had permitted it. Now his expression was a hard, cold mask, revealing nothing. It must be a another skill of his profession, she thought miserably, suddenly feeling like a defendant dragged before him.

The feeling intensified as he growled, "I asked you a question, and I want an answer. Why are you telling me this?"

Sarah swallowed, hard, absorbing the tension that radiated from him and feeling it all the way to her toes. "Because you have a right to know."

"Because I have a right to know." She watched him turn the words over in his mind, weighing them, measuring them on what yardstick she wasn't sure. "Not because you want to share a painful memory with me, or because we ran into the bastard at dinner some night and the subject came up naturally. No, because I have a *right* to know." The words became lethal weapons as they were ripped from his mouth, his icy control slipping a notch. "Are your teeth capped?"

The question threw Sarah off her already precarious balance. She met his angry gaze, half wishing it were still unreadable. "What?"

"Your teeth," he snapped. "Are they capped?"

"What difference does it make?"

"Don't you think I have a *right* to know about any and all of your biological imperfections? I've had a nice, long look at your body, and I can testify that it's free of scars, but what about inside? Is there anything else I can't see that I should know about?"

Hot tears welled just inside her lashes, and Sarah turned to stare at the porch screen, a pattern of gray lines against the black night. Brad's fingers clutched her chin and jerked her back to face his seething fury.

"What about me?" he demanded, his voice taunting. "Exactly how detailed a physical report should I be prepared to submit? Do you want to know about broken bones? Childhood diseases?"

Her jaw trembled in the cage of his fingers, shattering the words as she spoke them. "Why are you doing this? Why are you trying to hurt me?"

His eyes focused on her cheek. He slid his thumb up to halt the path of the tear slithering its way down, staring at it as if it were the first he'd ever seen. Sarah shuddered with relief as she saw the fight drain out of him and felt it in the fingers that turned from harsh to gentle on her face.

"I don't know," he said, his eyes closing briefly. "Probably because you hurt me. Childish, huh?"

Sarah reeled in confusion. This had all been to avoid hurting him, not the opposite. "I should have just kept it to myself. I wasn't being pushy; I just thought—"

"You thought right." His smile was weak, but it lit up Sarah's world like a Christmas tree. "It's not that you told me; it's the way you told me. Your reason for doing it." His eyes glittered incredulously. "Did you honestly think it would make a difference to me?"

"I couldn't afford to hope it wouldn't."

Brad groaned at the shaky admission and pulled her to him, nestling her against his chest as he lay back against the glider's deep cushions. His fingers slipped over the satin skin of her throat and shoulder. "Sarah"— her name became a rough purr—"are you so used to being disappointed?"

She pressed against his strong chest, finding the place that seemed to have been carved just for her. "I think the rest of my life would be one long disappointment if you walked away from me now."

He nuzzled the top of her head. "There's not a chance of my walking away—ever—and I plan to spend the rest of my life making sure you're never disappointed again."

The promise sent an intoxicating warmth rushing through her. Still, she couldn't let it rest until she was sure.

"Will I disappoint you?"

His arms tightened around her, telegraphing that he understood what she was really asking. "Never. You're the woman I love, Sarah. I don't have some preordained plan for my future that I'll try to plug you into. Our future will be what we make it, together. And we don't need to plan every step of it here and now." Gentle fingers cupped her chin, lifting it. His eyes glittered with tender promises. "Just know this: You are not lacking in anything I need. I fell head over heels in love with you because of who you are, not for what you might be able to give me someday in the future. All I'll ever need from you is in place, right here." His hand slid lower, framing the soft curve over her heart as gently as it had her face. "Just love me, Sarah."

Sarah brightened with sheer joy. "What about what's up here?" she asked, tapping her forehead.

"That could cause problems," he admitted with a heavy

sigh. "You worry too much."

On cue, her smile dimmed. She tilted her head back to see all of his face. "Brad, I still want to take things slowly. I want you to have time to think this all over when I'm not around."

He took advantage of their positions to nibble at her lips. "I don't plan on your ever not being around for long. Besides, maybe you should be doing the thinking. I'm not the one hitching wagons with a man who's about to wager everything he owns on a dream. Does the thought of bankruptcy make you queasy, love?"

She twisted around in his arms, bracing her hands on his broad shoulders. "Not half as queasy as the thought of you sticking with a job that doesn't make you happy out of a sense of duty."

"Sense of duty dies hard with us Chandlers."

Wry self-depreciation colored his words. In the past few days Sarah had learned a great deal about this man she loved. She'd also learned a lot about his family, including the ironclad sense of civic responsibility passed on from generation to generation of Chandlers as naturally as the blue blood running through their veins. The progression from ivy league university to law school to the bench to political office was steeped in family tradition. Helping him take the first step off that well-worn path was going to require a very deft touch.

"Brad, if that had been one of your sailing buddies, instead of Purini, who wanted to have a long talk with you tonight, where would we be right now?"

He grinned and swallowed the baited hook. "Probably sitting in some seedy waterfront bar talking sailboats."

"Just as I suspected. And what does that tell you?"

"That you're almost as smart as you are beautiful."

"Seriously, Brad." She resisted his maneuver to pull her closer.

"I am serious," he insisted, giving up the effort and lifting his head to circle the pulse spot at the base of her throat with his tongue instead.

A shiver coursed through her at the erotic touch. "Stop," she ordered. "We have to talk."

He complied, reluctantly releasing her from his arms so she could sit beside him. "Sarah, I could sit and listen to you talk for hours, but my hormones say you've got about three minutes, so make it fast."

"I just want you to know that I'm not some evil spirit trying to lure you away from your noble dedication to duty over the objections of your family. I know you're a good judge, and you'd be a good senator, too, but I love you, and your happiness is more important to me than anything else." Brad's smile encouraged her, making the words flow effortlessly. "I know how hard it can be to stop trying to live up to everyone else's idea of what you should be. Lord knows I flunked enough science courses in college before I decided to follow my own interests, instead of the ones my family said were right for me."

His hand stroked her hair. "Is that what put such distance between you and your family, love?"

Sarah glanced at him with wide eyes, surprised that he'd sensed something she held so close to her core. Yet she wasn't really surprised at all. She lowered her head to a shoulder that was warm and reassuringly solid. Long ago she'd come to terms with her family's disappointment in her, but the withholding of the approval she craved by the people she loved most still hurt.

"I suppose it has. At the time they were violently opposed to my switching majors from biology to English. Lately my work is a topic we touch on very lightly." Her shoulders lifted in a resigned shrug. "It's not so much that they come right out and say I'm a disappointment, just that I know I'm not a source of pride."

Brad's eyes were as loving as the hand gliding softly over the dark silk of her hair. "You are a source of pride to me, and a source of pleasure, of happiness. You become more to me with each passing day. Until you, I never seriously questioned that my career was the most important thing in my life. It won by default. I never knew there could be so much more."

"I was afraid to look for more," Sarah admitted quietly. "In my work I have complete control. It's safe, secure."

Brad didn't move or pull her closer, but the sudden intensity in his gaze tightened the web of intimacy around them. "So am I, Sarah."

Her eyes lit with wonder as they lifted to his. "I believe you are."

"How did we get so lucky?" he asked, his soft chuckle tickling her ear.

"Must live right, I guess."

Brad shook his head firmly. "It can't be that. I feel as though I've just started living right, and I don't plan on regressing."

She shifted to face him fully. "What you said before— about risking everything for a dream—does that mean you've made your decision?"

Eyes glittering with an excitement Sarah could feel, he nodded. "Yes. I'd just about made up my mind anyway, but talking with Purini at the party pushed me over the edge. There's no way I want to live the rest of my life according to the narrow ideal of what he and others like him think it ought to be. I kept telling myself it was selfish, and a crazy risk besides, to think about designing and building boats full time just because it would make me happy. Thanks to you, I don't feel that way any more." Sarah's breath caught in her throat at the mingling of gratitude and adoration in his eyes. "And you can forget all that garbage about luring me away from duty. Your enthusiasm and support have done for me what no one else ever has—sanctified my happiness as a reason for making the break—and I owe you for that."

"No." Shaking her head and smiling, Sarah reached

up and wrapped her arms around Brad's neck. "I only told you the truth. I see a passion and excitement in you when you're talking about your boats that's not there for anything else." She flushed as he lifted both dark eyebrows in a very insinuating manner. "Well, almost nothing else. You've spent your whole life excelling at other people's expectations, Brad. You deserve the chance to see if you can excel at your own."

"I'd much rather see if I can excel at yours." His husky tone and the smoldering green of his eyes told Sarah the three minutes he'd granted had run out, and she felt her pulse quicken in anticipation. "Tell me all you expect from a lover, Sarah."

The forthright command startled her. More comfortable with lovemaking than she'd ever dreamed she could be, she still felt awkward talking about it so openly, even with this man who'd spent hours learning how to pleasure every inch of her.

"You are all I expect," she told him truthfully, "and so much more."

His mouth came down on hers with a loving ferocity that unleashed something deep inside her. She responded to his demand with a wild one of her own, catching his tongue in a gentle suction, then giving chase as it retreated into the sweetness behind his parted lips. The sparks ignited by the powerful kiss sizzled along Sarah's nerves, swirling in her stomach, and lower, until everything inside seemed to melt, leaving only the need to receive his passion and the burning desire to repay him with her own.

His breath coming in rapid gusts, Brad lifted his head and ran his hands over her shoulders and back in a fevered caress before easing her into the corner of the glider.

"Don't move," he instructed, his voice a deep rasp.

Sarah's soft moan of protest faded to a smile as he swiftly lowered the bamboo shades, turning the porch into a private, softly glowing domain. His long stride

carried him back to stand before her, and with a tantalizing smile he pulled her to her feet. As he reached for
the gown's single clasp over one shoulder, Sarah saw
his hand tremble and felt a rush of emotion that she could
affect his strength to that degree. With Brad's urgent
help, the gown swished from her body to lie like a soft
raspberry cloud at her feet. Using his outstretched palms
for balance, she stepped from the gown, then held her
breath as he fell to his knees and eased her slip, pantyhose, and panties off at once.

It was Brad's turn to catch his breath. For long moments he knelt in silence, staring at the shadows and
highlights cast on her body by the lamp's amber glow.
Slowly, reverently, as if afraid she might disintegrate at
his touch, he moved his hands over her, barely touching
her breasts, the slight convexity of her stomach. His arms
looped around her hips, pulling her closer so he could
nuzzle the pale satin of her skin before wordlessly guiding
her back down on the glider. He shed his own clothes
impatiently, then fell to his knees before her once more,
the lamplight flowing over him, gilding the ridges and
muscular swells of his hard body.

The only sound was the faint rustle of the lilac bush
brushing against the screen as its branches swayed in the
lazy spring breeze. The sweet perfume of its blooms
wafted through the screens, scenting the warm night air.
Sarah leaned forward, offering her lips to Brad in a kiss
that went from delicate to hungry in a flash. Still consuming her mouth, he moved his hands over her in a
wisp of a caress, leaving each part of her he touched
aching for more. When his warm fingers feathered the
sensitive skin of her inner thighs, Sarah made a soft,
inarticulate sound and shifted on the cushion, inviting
deeper intimacy.

"Easy, love," Brad murmured in gentle denial of the
tacit command.

Gripping her hips firmly, he pulled her to the edge of

the seat and held her there while he concentrated his attentions on her ear, tonguing it gently, his breath a hot mist that flooded her senses. Sarah twisted in his hold, shivering and burning up at the same time. With excruciating thoroughness and lips that felt like hot silk, he wandered over her throat and shoulders, leaving a trail of liquid fire behind.

Sarah could feel her desire escalating steadily, growing from a warm, pleasant glow to a frantic throbbing that spread from deep inside to ignite every fiber of her being with primitive longing. When he slid lower, using his teeth and tongue to tease her breasts until the nipples hardened in response, she trembled against him with a small gasp. Brad's soft laugh was full of pleasure as he moved lower still, nibbling his way along the line of her hipbones, dipping a slow kiss in her navel. When he gently parted her thighs and sought the damp, silky hollow between, she arched, excited and frightened at once.

"Brad . . ."

"Shh." His breath was a teasing burst of warmth. "Please don't stop me, Sarah. I *want* to give you more than you expect. I want to know all of you. God, you're beautiful."

Drawing comfort and confidence from the love that shaded his gravelly plea, Sarah surrendered to the magic of his possession. His name fell from her lips in a loving chant as she soared higher and higher, the sensations spiraling within growing deeper and stronger until they erupted in a spasm of pleasure that left her gasping and clutching his shoulders for support in a world that his touch had set spinning around her.

Brad pulled her against him, holding her until her world righted itself, stroking her skin, which was covered with a faint sheen of perspiration. Gradually his touches grew provocative once more, and his lips moved on hers, coaxing, urging a response she'd mistakenly thought had been drained. With a careful movement he lifted the glider cushion, and her, to the floor.

"It's not that I'm not adventurous," he explained in laughing response to her questioning glance, "but I prefer to create my own undulation."

He did, first with movements that were slow and flowing, then with a powerful surge Sarah matched with a fury all her own. She hadn't thought she could feel passion that intense so soon again, and when it passed she lay curled in Brad's strong arms, savoring an all-new sense of completeness that settled over her like a clear spring morning.

Chapter Eight

IN THE WEEK that followed, Sarah saw Brad morning, night, and even most afternoons. The days grew into a collage of precious memories: Brad, face into the wind, working the sails of his boat with such flowing ease he seemed a part of its sleek, polished form; Brad, looking big and out of place and incredibly beautiful against the lacy, feminine backdrop of her bedroom; Brad, bare-chested and grease-smudged, mumbling dire threats from under the hood of her uncooperative old car.

On Wednesday he dragged her to that waterfront bar to meet his sailing buddies. It turned out to be not so seedy after all, and the other men welcomed Sarah with friendly warmth and enough surprised expressions to re-affirm that she held a place in Brad's life that wasn't given carelessly.

On Thursday Brad returned the favor by agreeing to have dinner with Julie and her latest appendage, a mid-dleweight boxer who seemed to have boxing confused with wrestling and thought Julie was his opponent. Brad declared the evening a valuable remedial lesson on all the reasons he hadn't double-dated since high school. Always when they were with others there were the subtle touches, the private looks that conveyed a mutual longing to be alone again.

On Friday he told her he would have to be away the whole following week.

"That's fine," Sarah said nobly, her mouth frozen in a bright smile that didn't come close to reaching her eyes. Years of practice aided the process of internalizing the reason he was leaving her. "I told you that you needed some time away from me to think. Things have been moving much too quickly."

They sat facing each other, shoulder deep in bubbles in Brad's oversized bathtub. A hell of a place to break the news that her life would soon slip back into tedious monotony, thought Sarah. Oddly enough, it had never seemed tedious or monotonous until Brad spilled into it like sunshine on a cold winter day.

He shook his head, his expression indulgently amused, and leaned closer to paint her shoulders with lemon-scented foam. "Things would have to move a hell of a lot faster to suit me. And they will, just as soon as I take care of one leftover responsibility. I have to go to Boston to give a series of lectures at Harvard Law School," he explained briefly. "If it wasn't a long overdue favor to an old friend, nothing could tear me away from you for three entire days."

"You said a week," Sarah reminded him, hating the glum sound of her own voice.

"Right, but if I leave early Monday morning and start back right after my lecture on Friday, that leaves only three days I actually won't see you." He looked extremely proud of his ingenuity, but Sarah could feel needles of guilt piercing her happiness at his revised schedule.

"I'm sorry I sounded naggy," she told him, "as if I expect you to punch a clock."

His broad grin and glittering eyes made for a very

convincing parody of a sexy leer as he drawled, "I'll punch your clock anytime, sweetheart." Then, not fazed in the least by her laughing groan, he added, "Besides, I told you already, I've done all the thinking about us that I plan to do. If you want to dissect our relationship on some lofty, cerebral plane, be my guest. But as of three o'clock this afternoon my resignation was official, and I became just a simple working man."

"At the risk of shattering your blue-collar illusions, I have to point out that simple working men don't own sprawling estates on one of the most exclusive streets in the country."

His mouth curved wryly. "Neither will I very shortly if my folks are half as adept at predicting the future as they are at planning it."

Sarah's eyes widened with surprise and curiosity. "You told them?"

"This afternoon." He leaned back against the gleaming chocolate-brown tile wall, looking very calm and cheerful for a survivor of what Sarah suspected had been a highly vocal clash of wills.

Half afraid the nonchalance might be a facade to conceal his real feelings, she asked cautiously, "What did they say?"

"About what I expected," he replied, seemingly more interested in the rivulets of warm water he was squeezing from a facecloth onto the slope of her breasts. "My mother said I must be out of my mind to throw away my bright, promising future on a whim."

"That's all?"

He tilted his head with a smile of tantalizing mischief. "Actually, there was probably a whole lot more, but sometime after learning that I was turning my back on my heritage to chase after a pipe dream, and that a fool and his money are soon parted, I propped the receiver on the sofa and left to pick you up at work."

"Brad! You mean you just dropped the phone and

walked out while your mother was still talking?"

"My mother and father," he corrected matter-of-factly. "About forty-five minutes into the argument Father grabbed the extension so they could coerce me in stereo. In all probability they're still at it, talking so fast and furiously they haven't even noticed I left." His eyes narrowed in interest. "Do you think they can hear us splashing?"

Sarah shook her head, trying not to laugh, not entirely sure that what he was saying wasn't the outrageous truth. "Brad Chandler, you're heartless."

"That's a fact." He dropped the facecloth and ran his fingers over the slick surface of her skin, carefully avoiding the peaks of her breasts, which tautened anyway. "I have been since the night of our infamous blind date. It's all worked out very well though; I ended up with something much more valuable than that old heart."

"A new bionic one?" Sarah teased, her hint of breathlessness directly attributable to the skilled movements of his palms.

"Even better—I have a woman who can cast spells."

The wicked glint in his eyes suggested he would be quite capable in that area himself, but Sarah played along, feigning astonishment. "No! You mean a real witch?"

In the warm depths of the water his hands found her and pulled her into the cradle of his hard thighs. "That's right." His husky voice was as stirring to her senses as his slippery touch was. "C'mon, Sarah, bewitch me."

Sarah used the time Brad was away to catch up on all the work she'd fallen so far behind on during the past few weeks. She put the finishing touches on the upcoming issue Friday morning and made a mental note to tell Brad when he returned that evening that he wouldn't be gracing its pages. He never mentioned the article when they were together, and Sarah hoped it was because he found the prospect unsettling despite his determination to be supportive of her. However, on the off chance that being overlooked might bruise his ego, she'd refrained from spoiling their lengthy, late-night phone calls with the news.

The nightly calls had been the one bright spot in the whole week. Although not nearly as good as having him with her, talking for hours on the phone had a special intimacy all its own. It allowed them the luxury of sharing childhood trivia and secrets long forgotten, and of interweaving their dreams for the future in a way that wasn't possible when they were in the same room and the heat of their passion ultimately overrode casual conversation. In a tongue-in-cheek manner that couldn't quite cloak the remnants of loneliness from the woman who loved him, Brad related tales of growing up in a world where servants had starring roles and his own parents played bit parts. Sarah could see so clearly how the needs of the man sprang from the experience of the little boy, and she vowed to spend the rest of her life drowning Brad in love to make up for what his parents hadn't given him... and maybe a little for what she wasn't able to give.

Brad listened to her as well as she revealed to another human being for the first time ever how much she had hated growing up the black sheep in the family, how she'd alternated between trying desperately to fulfill her parents' expectations and resenting them for it. She spoke hesitantly, wondering if someone like Brad, who had always been number one at all the right things, could ever understand the layers of inferiority built up from years of trying with your heart and soul to win the respect of others, only to discover you just don't have what it takes.

"It's not you who failed, Sarah," he said softly when she trailed off with an abrupt, self-conscious laugh. "It's them. They failed to see how special you are. I guess in some ways it can be just as lonely growing up in the middle of a big family as it is growing up all alone."

"I was never lonely exactly," Sarah explained, feeling a trifle guilty as she remembered there had been lots of good times despite the relentless underlying pressure to conform. "But I never felt special. A little odd, maybe, but never special."

"But you *are* special, and if it takes me the next fifty years, I'm going to prove that to you. I miss you, Sarah."

Sarah smiled. Magic. The man could perform magic even over telephone lines. "I miss you, too, more than I ever thought possible. I miss everything about you."

His chuckle was heartwarmingly familiar, a verbal caress. "Like the way I use up all the hot water in your shower and reorganize your kitchen cupboards?"

"Actually, I've been practicing the art of selective recall. I'm concentrating on missing all the good things: the way you look, the sound of your voice." She bit her lip, smiling through a sudden attack of the shyness Brad was slowly freeing her from. "I even miss the way you taste."

"God, Sarah," he groaned, sounding as if his mouth was pressed to the phone, "Don't say things like that to me when I'm too far away to do anything about it."

"We can dream," she ventured.

"That only makes it worse." She thrilled to the desperation in his even deeper than normal tone. "If I left right now I could be at your place in less than two hours."

Sarah glanced at the clock by her bed, common sense warring with her yearning to encourage him to come. "That would make it after one, and you'd have to leave here by six. You wouldn't get much sleep."

"I wouldn't be coming to sleep."

She sighed, yielding to her common sense and cursing it at the same time. "No. I'd worry all day tomorrow that you were falling asleep at the lectern or, worse, at the wheel of your car. It's only one more day. I can make it."

* * *

That turned out to be a classic example of easier said than done. She hadn't known then that Friday would be the longest day of her entire life, suddenly sprouting extra hours all over the place, the hands on her office clock standing defiantly still no matter how many times she checked it.

"Aren't you afraid all that staring will wear it out?" asked Melanie, pointedly following Sarah's gaze to the offending clock.

"No, but I am seriously considering *throwing* it out," she retorted. "I think it's slow."

"It's fast," Melanie informed her, "and you're making me as jittery as you seem to be. Why don't you leave early? After all, you did come in nearly two hours early this morning."

Sarah shrugged defensively. "I couldn't sleep."

"So go home and take a nap." In a very unsubtle manner Melanie handed Sarah her purse. "Then when you wake up you can kill time taking a bath, painting your nails, and staring at your own clock for a while."

Sarah laughingly let herself be driven out of her own office. She knew anything as relaxed as a nap was out of the question, but a bath didn't sound like a bad idea. At least there was no clock in the bathroom to tick away the agonizing homestretch. But when she arrived home to find her parking spot occupied by a gleaming black BMW, she knew a bath was not at all what she wanted. She was out of the car and up the steps in seconds; Brad had the door open even quicker. He met her on the front steps and swept her up in his arms, carrying her into the house and kicking the door shut behind them like the hero in a romantic comedy. Sarah told him so.

"I don't feel romantic," he murmured without interrupting the path of urgent kisses leading from her throat to her waiting lips. "I feel hungry and passionate. How do you feel?"

His touch was playing havoc with her thoughts, stealing them right out from under her. "Hungry and passionate," she echoed absently. "I'd say that sums it up nicely."

His laugh formed against her ear, a low, rich sound she heard as well as felt. "Good. I spent the whole ride home in dire fear you'd want us to spend the evening with friends or going to a movie."

"Well, now that you mention it, there is a great film—"

"Quiet, woman," he ordered, but his voice was gentle, the smile curving his mouth mesmerizing, and she watched, transfixed, as it came closer, closer.

They kissed fully, as if one kiss could recapture the week they'd lost. Brad's lips and tongue moved against hers, inviting, demanding, then surrendering fully so Sarah could learn all over again the hot, varied textures of his open mouth. The sweet hunger grew, sizzling back and forth until a kiss was no longer enough. Nothing would be enough until they came together so completely they forgot to breathe, melting in a flame so torrid they wouldn't know where one of them left off and the other began.

Still holding her in his arms, Brad strode toward the bedroom. The tipped blinds held the afternoon sunlight at bay as they fell together on her bed. Sarah trembled as he undressed her, interrupting himself often to feed the slow burn of their passion with movements that were a silken blend of power and grace. He held himself from her only long enough to shed his own clothes, and then the world altered crazily, narrowing until it held only the two of them, expanding to hold the wildness of their need for each other, the fullness of their love.

Afterward Sarah lay with her head on his hard chest, finding it more comfortable than an eiderdown pillow. She trailed her fingers lightly over his skin, relishing her right to do so. She traced the tendons in his forearm, which flexed in rhythm with his strokes along the curve of her hip. Her fingers swept across the muscular swell of his upper arm to his chest, ruffling the dark hair that curled there, following the ridges of muscle, finally coming to rest on the hard plane of his stomach.

Love for him washed over her in dense, languorous waves that compounded and intensified the lingering satisfaction from their lovemaking. She loved all of him— every hard line, every masculine angle, and all the thoughts and dreams and emotions residing beneath his perfect surface that made him the man he was. She smiled and stretched with feline contentment at the thought of the weekend stretching lazily before them, promising a splendor that would obliterate the bleakness of the past five days.

"A movie," she scoffed incredulously. Looking up, she found his eyes on her, warm, their green hue smoky with love. "How could you possibly think I'd miss this for a movie? The truth is I think we should spend the next two days right where we are, except for brief forays into the kitchen and bath, of course." She teased his thigh by rubbing against it lightly with her own, soon discovering that her seductive gesture was a double-edged sword. "On second thought, maybe we could skip the kitchen altogether."

Nuzzling the top of her head, Brad swept his fingers across her back, bathing her skin with the magic of his touch. His soft chuckle faded into a heavy, strangely regretful sigh. "That sounds fantastic, love, but I'm afraid it might be a little crowded."

"Not at all." She smiled up at him provocatively. "Haven't you ever heard? Two's company."

"And three's a crowd," he finished dryly. "So what does that make thirteen?"

Her smile dissolved in a cloud of apprehension. "A baker's dozen. Why do you ask?"

He sighed again, tightening his hold on her briefly. "I'm afraid it's another leftover duty call—a promise I made to Tommy and had forgotten all about until I called Nancy a few days ago to check on things over there.".

Sarah hated the instinct that caused her involuntary stiffening. Was she jealous of Tommy? Or of Nancy? Or simply of the fact that Brad felt he had to call to check on them if he was away for even a few days?

"Of course. Saturdays," she said, hearing the strain permeating her carefully bright tone. "I should have remembered that you always spend them with Tommy."

"That's not a hard and fast rule," Brad said slowly, his eyes on her narrowed, concerned. "That's usually been the most convenient time for both of us in the past, but my schedule with Tommy will bend to your wishes. I've already told him that."

Love for him flooded her senses in a dizzying rush, and hard on its heels came a humiliating guilt that she'd been reluctant to share so small a part of him. "I'm sorry. I want you to spend tomorrow with Tommy. Truly."

"It's not just tomorrow, love. I promised Tommy months ago that I'd take his Cub Scout troop on an overnight camping trip. That's where the baker's dozen comes in."

"A dozen Cub Scouts?" she asked numbly, feeling the promise of their golden weekend shattering.

"No, ten scouts and Nancy and me and . . ."

She twisted from his arms and stood with a harsh laugh she couldn't suppress. She managed to shove one arm into her rose silk robe before he grabbed her wrist.

"Where do you think you're going?" he demanded, rising to his knees in the center of the bed, his body naked, magnificent, a distracting reminder she could definitely do without.

"I think we should get dressed, maybe go take in a movie." It was a petty blow, but she was too hurt to care.

"The hell we will." The savage-sounding oath was barely out of his mouth when she was unceremoniously hauled back into a sitting position on the bed and held there with a strength that made a farce of her effort to pull away. "What's gotten into you? Are you really that angry about the camping trip? I knew you'd be disappointed, especially this weekend. I am, too, but I did promise—"

"Angry?" she interrupted, barely parting her clenched teeth to speak. "Disappointed? Why should I be? Just because I've spent all week missing you—counting the damn hours until you got back—and you have the nerve to stroll in here and take me to bed and *then* remember to tell me you'll be spending the rest of the weekend with Nancy."

"Not just Nancy," he countered, the perplexity in the depths of his eyes giving way to a mingling of disbelief and burgeoning amusement. "That's it—you're jealous."

"Of course I'm not," she said none too convincingly.

He rolled her down onto her back with a hug, his laugh tinged with relief. "Don't be embarrassed about it. If I thought you were going camping for the weekend with another man, I'd be more than jealous. I'd be homicidal."

"How reassuring." She held herself like a sheet of ice in his arms. "That doesn't change the fact that you're going."

"We're going," he corrected, dimples slashing his cheeks as he watched her eyes cloud with confusion. "I don't want us to spend another two days apart any more than you do. This won't be exactly the way I fantasized this weekend, but at least we'll be together."

Sarah felt the anger draining out of her and a sort of relieved happiness seeping back in. "Just you and me and Nancy and the scouts?"

Brad nodded. "Right—a baker's dozen." He was lying on top of her, his upper body supported on his outstretched arms, the rest of it a sweet temptation. "You don't look exactly thrilled at the prospect."

"No," she agreed, breaking into a slow smile, "thrilled is not the word that comes first to mind." She pressed her fingertips to his lips before he had a chance to speak. "Don't ask; I never say those kinds of words in mixed company. I will tell you this thought: Camping with you and Nancy and company is probably the next to the last way I'd choose to spend this weekend."

"At least there's something you consider worse," Brad noted optimistically.

Lifting up, Sarah brushed her lips across his in an unmistakable invitation and murmured, "Uh-huh. Having you and Nancy go without me."

They put her plan of restricted movement into practice for the remainder of the night, venturing forth only to stage a midnight raid on the refrigerator. One hunger satisfied, they returned to the sanctuary of her bed to wrestle with one that proved to be insatiable. Sleeping in short stretches, interrupted frequently and at length by storms born of desire, they finally woke to a day that was clear and pink—depressingly perfect for camping.

"I prayed all night for rain," Brad groaned, his body a shaft of heated steel curling around her back.

Sarah twisted to face him with a wry smile. "Brad, I was with you all night; you didn't have time to breathe, much less pray."

His hands bracketed her hips and lifted her over him so she straddled his hips, down low. The contact was electric and ever-new, demanding phenomenal restraint for Sarah to keep from melting and pouring over him like liquid fire.

"Do you want to argue details," he asked in a voice husky with renewed passion, "Or do you want to take advantage of our last moments of freedom?"

She bent in a misleading gesture of compliance, only to twist off him and break for the bathroom, calling back a sassy, "Neither. I want to enjoy the last private, civilized shower I'll probably have for days."

The shower ended up being not at all private and only faintly civilized, but they still managed to pick up the truck Brad had borrowed for the occasion and made it to Nancy's, the official rallying point, almost on schedule. It was a half hour ride to Fort Weatherhill in the nearby town of Jamestown, a state-run park that was a meandering collection of tidy campsites, small ponds, and densely wooded areas crisscrossed by mazelike paths. The campsite Brad had reserved weeks earlier was located well off the road, an oasis of sweet-scented clover ringed by towering pines that made Sarah long to be sharing it with him alone.

It was a desire not motivated by selfishness alone, she admitted to herself as they all pitched in to unload the mountain of camping paraphernalia from the back of the pickup. Revealing the truth about her inability to have children and Brad's lovingly supportive response had stoked a new feeling of self-worth inside her, but it hadn't completely obliterated all the old, deep-seated insecurities. That would take time, and Sarah only hoped whatever happened over the next two days wouldn't threaten the progress she had made so far. More than anything she wanted to meet Brad here, on his own terms, and prove to both of them that she could be a partner in every facet of his life.

It was a task Sarah knew she approached with minimal skill, her lack of experience around children exceeded only by her unfamiliarity with the great outdoors. Actually, her idea of roughing it was a fully equipped Winnebago and a portable screen house, and she'd never felt the slightest inclination to undertake even that—a fact that became painfully obvious during the phase of the outing Brad referred to as setting up camp.

He came and stood beside her as she unpacked the food cartons, painstakingly arranging the boxes and packages on one of the picnic tables. "Sarah, this can wait until you've pitched your tent."

"I already did—right over there where you said to."

He glanced at the spot she indicated and broke into a grin. "When I told you to pitch it over there I didn't mean it literally."

"How did you mean it?" she asked, not liking his grin half as much as she usually did.

"I meant *pitch* it, not pitch it." The inflection he gave the word varied, as did the accompanying hand signals.

"Oh, that's much clearer," she drawled with a sarcastically sweet smile.

"Sarah, by pitch it, I meant for you to set it up." The condescending explanation rankled more than his grinning had.

"Then you should have said so," she returned coolly, dropping the bag of hamburger rolls she was holding back into the carton and turning on her heel. "In case you haven't noticed, I'm not a cub scout."

She stomped over to her tent, feeling too indignant to appreciate the low-pitched, "I noticed. Believe me, I noticed," he directed at her retreating back. It would have been perfect—poetic justice—if she could have casually tossed the small tent up in no time flat and returned to unpacking groceries. Unfortunately, she discovered to her utter disgust, life in the wilderness is seldom perfect. Or fair. There wasn't even a role model to point her in the right direction. When, in a burst of unabashed machismo, Brad had announced that he planned to spread his sleeping bag under the stars, ten adoring little heads had nodded in enthusiastic agreement. She and Nancy would share the dubious honor of sleeping in the sole pup tent, *if* she ever managed to get it up. She was still struggling with the unfamiliar ropes and poles when Brad passed her, lugging a heavy cooler.

"Having a little trouble?" he inquired, panting from his many long trips back to the truck.

"Nothing I can't handle."

He shifted his grip on the cooler, and Sarah watched with fascination the play of muscles beneath his faded, sweat-drenched chambray shirt. The memories it stirred were balm to her ruffled pride.

"Sarah, have you ever been camping before?"

She met his mildly amused gaze with a small, rueful shrug. "Never."

"Then it's no disgrace to admit you need a hand putting up that tent."

She smiled up at him. "I need a hand."

"No problem." Smiling back, he shifted his grip again and took a step toward the center of camp. "I'll send one of the boys over to help you right away."

One of the boys, Sarah fumed, annoyance flaring anew.

"How gallant of you," she finally thought to mumble, but he was too far away to hear.

Determined not to strike out so early in the game, she forced a carefree smile and held it while eight-year-old Jason Rutgers pitched her tent in a grand total of seven minutes. He probably could have done it faster if he hadn't had to rely on her to reach the top of the center pole for him.

By the time she'd stowed hers and Nancy's gear inside the tent, the other woman had finished unpacking the food and was helping Brad set up a cooking area. Reluctant to butt in on what was clearly an efficient two-person operation and feeling awkward standing there watching them work, she scanned the campsite, where one group of boys was already tossing around a football while another, smaller group sat idly by. It was a relief when Brad did what she couldn't do for herself—found something to occupy her time.

"Sarah, if you wouldn't mind, those guys could use a guide to help them gather some firewood."

He nodded at the boys sitting nearby without taking his eyes off her. They burned through her faded jeans and red jersey, gleaming with unqualified approval for the first time since that morning. Sarah had no illusions that it was because of her camping skills, but at the moment it hardly mattered. When he looked at her that way she'd be willing to search for dry kindling in a hurricane if he asked her to.

"Sure. Any specific instructions, great leader?"

He smiled, taking the flip query as lightly as it was intended. "As a matter of fact, there are. Don't bother with anything too green or too damp. And don't split up, and don't go too far—keep this clearing in sight."

"I think I'm sorry I asked," she groaned, heading into the woods trailed by four little shadows.

It had been a dry spring so far, making it easy to find wood that wasn't too green or too damp, and before long all five pairs of arms were overflowing.

"Sarah, my wood is all slipping," complained a little boy named Joey, the smallest of the troop.

"Mine, too," echoed a second voice, followed closely by the others.

Sarah looked around, frowning. "I suppose I should have thought to bring something to carry it in." She tried to visualize the combined contents of their arms and made a wild guess that it wasn't enough to keep a good size campfire burning all evening. "I know, let's dump this load right here and keep going; then we can make two trips back to camp with it. Brad sure will be proud when he sees how much we found," she added to tip the scales in favor of her suggestion.

They kept walking, Sarah taking pains to note landmarks along the path as the campsite disappeared behind them. She had no intention of getting lost in the woods and was just about to give the word that they'd collected enough when a freckle-spattered redhead named Christopher let out a loud yelp of pain. She dashed around the cluster of shrubs separating them and dropped to her knees by his side.

"Christopher, what's the matter? Are you okay?"

He was whimpering loudly and clutching his right thigh with both hands. "Something bit me," he cried, "It hurts."

"Oh, honey, that's awful." She gave his shoulders a quick squeeze in what she hoped was a comforting manner. Judging by the escalation of his sobs, she was way off base. "Let me take a look."

"No!" He pulled away from her. "Don't touch me. You're not my mother. I want my mother."

Hunched over, crying in great heartbreaking gasps, he drew forth from Sarah an untempered flow of sympathy, and she searched desperately for some way to help him.

"Chris, if you'll just let me see your leg, maybe—"

"No! It hurts too bad," he wailed.

"Chris, what happened?"

Sarah didn't know who looked more relieved to hear the crisp, efficient sound of Nancy's voice—her or the child limping into the newcomer's open arms. Nancy gathered the little boy close and soothed him with gentle words until the sobs faded and he agreed to let her examine his leg.

"A bee sting," she announced promptly. She dipped the tail of her shirt into a nearby stream and wiped it over the red lump on Chris's leg to ease the pain until they could get him back to camp and the first-aid kit.

Sarah hadn't realized how shaken she was by the incident until she stood and felt her legs tremble beneath her. She was leaning against a tree, waiting for her equilibrium to return, when she heard Nancy's cheerful tone drop to a no-nonsense command.

"Todd, don't move. Stay right where you are."

While Sarah looked on in confusion, the little boy stopped in his tracks in the middle of some low foliage, then obediently followed Nancy's step-by-step instructions in walking back to the path.

"That's a patch of poison ivy," she explained to Sarah

when he was safely out. "Did any of the other kids walk through there?"

"I'm not sure," Sarah replied. She'd been so busy noting landmarks and counting heads she hadn't had time to notice who was walking where—even if the prospect of poison ivy had occurred to her.

"Well, there's one sure way to find out," Nancy said, her smile warm, nonjudgmental. "We'll ask them. These guys are old enough to know where they've been walking and if they're susceptible to poison ivy. The least we can do is alert their poor mothers to the possibility of it when we drop them off tomorrow."

She took a quick poll, getting varied responses. "One definite, one maybe, and one smart kid. That leaves only Joey." Nancy looked around briefly, then frowned. "Where *is* Joey?"

"He was right here. I counted heads just before Chris yelled." Sarah could feel her legs tremble again. "He has to be here."

She began running, several yards in one direction, then another, calling his name over and over.

"Sarah!" Nancy shouted after her. "That isn't going to help. Let's get Chris and the others back to the campsite. They can wait there while we split up and look for him."

"No." Fear rose inside Sarah, making it hard to swallow. Fear for the little boy she had lost out here and fear of having to face Brad's reaction to such stupidity. "He can't be far. You go on back. I have to find him."

"Sarah, no. We can cover more ground faster if we get Brad to help. Besides, he can yell louder than you and I together."

It became a moot point. Brad had come running, trailed by the other boys, at the sound of all their hollering. Nancy briefly outlined the situation, but before Brad had a chance to bark out instructions, Joey came ambling around a giant elm tree.

"Did you call me, Sarah?" he asked innocently. "I found a terrific pile of wood way over there." He gestured behind him with the long, gnarled branch he was carrying. "Look how big this one is."

The other kids descended on Joey en masse, teasing and berating him for getting lost like a baby. Shushing them, Nancy very firmly reminded Joey of the first rule of camping: Stick together. Sarah saw and heard the commotion through a suffocating fog of emotions. She sensed more than saw Brad standing beside her, his arm hard and warm across her shoulders, and then it all dissolved in the sound of low, broken sobs. This time they were her own.

Dimly she heard Brad say something to Nancy and her quick agreement as she began herding the kids back through the woods, leaving them alone. The tears subsided as quickly as they had come, leaving Sarah with a hollow feeling she was afraid would pierce much deeper before it was through. Under Brad's gentle guidance, she rested her back against the rough, scarred trunk of a nearby tree.

His strong brown fingers dusted her cheeks. "You've had one rough day, haven't you? First the tent, then Joey."

"You forgot the bee sting and the poison ivy," she added wearily.

"Do you want to run that by me again?"

Compassion radiated from him in warm penetrating beams, but it wasn't enough to stem the flood of misery inside her. Not nearly enough. Briefly she filled him in on the minor disasters he'd missed and watched him shrug carelessly.

"That's kids for you—always wandering away or into something they shouldn't. They'll survive."

"No thanks to me."

He tipped her face up and studied it with worried eyes. "You're not blaming yourself for any of this, are you?

Never mind—I can see that's exactly what you're doing. Sarah, love"—he rested his palms against the tree on either side of her shoulders and nuzzled the top of her head—"those things could have happened to anyone."

"All in one afternoon?"

"Stranger things have happened."

"They wouldn't have happened to you . . . or Nancy."

"We've been around children a lot more than you have. And we've both been camping before."

Together? The question slid automatically into Sarah's mind. She thanked God she wasn't unhinged enough to blurt it out.

"It was a mistake to bring you along this weekend," Brad said bluntly.

Sarah jerked her gaze away from the blatant regret in his. "I seem to be involving you in a long series of mistakes."

"I make my own mistakes, Sarah." His voice was firm, as were the fingers that turned her face back to his. "And the reason I said bringing you was one is because it wasn't fair to you. I steamrolled you into this whole thing without even bothering to ask if you'd ever been camping, or if you even wanted to come."

"I wanted to come."

"Past tense?" he probed, his slight smile tinged with an anxiousness that should have thrilled her.

Sarah took a deep breath, determined to salvage what remained of the weekend, for his sake and the kids'. What had to be settled between them could wait another day.

"Past and present." Her lips stretched into what she hoped looked like a smile. "I should start to get the hang of all this by, say, the time we break camp tomorrow."

"Break camp?" he echoed, his own smile breaking out full force. "You're beginning to sound like a pro already."

"Well, shall we go see how good this pro is at rustling up some grub?"

Brad stilled her slight movement, keeping her caged against the tree. "Not so fast. They'll survive without us for another few minutes. I, on the other hand, may not survive being close to you all night and not being able to have you."

The consuming sensuality of his mood was contagious. In this, at least, they were compatible, Sarah thought, feeling the first stirrings of excitement close to the spot where his hard belly rubbed hers.

"I don't think you have any choice," she pointed out wistfully.

"Try telling that to my libido."

"I wouldn't even try. As I recall, your libido has a mind of its own."

He smiled wickedly. "A one-track mind at that."

"Why do I suddenly feel like the helpless heroine tied to that track?"

"Just naturally perceptive, I suppose." His eyes darkened until they were more black than green, signaling that he was rapidly losing patience with playing. "Don't worry, love; for this weekend at least, I'll see that you're rescued in the nick of time."

Being rescued from his loving ranked down there with camping on her list of desires, and feeling his mouth press across hers with a passion she knew was barely leashed, Sarah wondered if either of them would have the willpower to stop in the nick of time. His long fingers twisted through her dark, tangled hair, cushioning her head from the tree's rough bark as his tongue stormed her mouth.

Excitement flared inside Sarah at the sweetness of his ravishment, and she surrendered to it, refusing to think about what lay beyond the next silken thrust, and the next, and the next. When he did break away it was to search out the curves of her ear, tasting, exploring with a boldness that was as untamed as the lush foliage around them.

He kissed her hair, then the graceful curve of her throat, finally returning to whisper one word against her glistening lips. "More."

Thinking that raspy utterance must be close to what a dragon would sound like if it could purr, Sarah somehow summoned up the restraint to decline. "You've already had way too much. As it is we're going to have to walk very slowly on the way back so you'll have time to . . . pull yourself together."

He followed her pointed gaze down to the unusually rounded area below his belt and smiled ruefully. "Do you at least give rain checks?"

"That depends," she drawled, moving away from the tree and him. "Do I have to lead the firewood brigade again tomorrow?"

He laughed as he put his arm around her waist, their bodies sliding together perfectly. "No. As a matter of fact, you didn't have to do it today. I always bring along a grill and charcoal. We'll light a small fire later just for the sake of tradition, but gathering wood is mainly a ruse to keep the kids out of the way."

The kids and her, Sarah thought, but she didn't say it. What difference did it make? It was, after all, a small thing, but it underscored exactly how poorly she fit into Brad's life, how totally useless she really was to him.

Chapter Nine

THE REST OF the weekend passed uneventfully, to Sarah's relieved amazement. After its calamitous beginnings she wouldn't have been a bit surprised if Christopher had turned out to be fatally allergic to bee stings and the kindling she'd collected spontaneously combusted, starting a history-making forest fire.

Actually, a large part of the credit for such smooth sailing was hers. She took great pains to stay out of everyone's way, avoiding all involvement in things she didn't know how to do—which turned out to be almost everything related to kids or camping. She did manage to smile perpetually, as if she were having the time of her life, even while washing ten little mess kits at a cold-water pump.

All in all, surviving the entire episode proved an exhausting task, and by the time Brad drove her home late Sunday evening she felt more as though she'd survived a grueling two-day endurance test than a weekend of camping fun. When he automatically started to follow her into the house she stopped him, smiling wearily.

"I'm kind of tired tonight, Brad."

He closed the door behind him, his eyes riveted on her face. "So am I, so let's not play games."

Sarah had been so preoccupied with her own misery during the short ride home from Nancy's that she hadn't questioned Brad's silence. Now, looking at him closely, she realized it had its roots in something much more complex than fatigue, and she knew instinctively that he was in no mood to hear what would have to be said sooner or later.

Tossing her overnight bag on the sofa, she followed it down and propped her feet on the hassock in an effort to appear carefree. "I won't argue with that. I've had my fill of games this weekend—badminton, king of the mountain—"

"Charades?" Brad interrupted, his voice distinctly cool.

When she just stared up at him, trying to weigh the intent of his query, he continued. "Isn't that what your cheerful little performance this weekend has been? A charade? Ever since we walked out of those woods together yesterday afternoon you've been smiling like a damn Barbie doll, and been almost as talkative."

"That's not true!" she snapped, knowing it was.

He glowered at her with an impatient wave of his arm.

"Don't lie to me, Sarah. I know you inside and out, and I damn well know when you're enjoying yourself and when you're gritting your teeth so hard you could spit enamel. What I want to know is why."

She straightened on the sofa and ran shaky fingers through her hair, reluctant to tangle with him when they were both bordering on exhaustion. "I've already told you I'm not much of an outdoors woman. I just didn't want to spoil the trip for the kids."

"Very commendable." He nodded stiffly. "But that doesn't explain why you avoided me like the plague, or why you brushed off all my attempts to talk to you alone, *or* why you barricaded yourself inside that tent at sundown, leaving me sitting by the fire with Nancy when all I wanted was to hold you."

The tirade that had started out harsh and accusing ended on a soft, almost pleading note that threatened to undermine all the resolve Sarah had spent the last two days cultivating.

"There is no simple explanation," she began dejectedly. "I avoided talking to you because I needed to talk to you so badly, and I knew we couldn't be alone, uninterrupted."

"We are now," he said simply.

She lifted one shoulder, a small weary gesture. "It just isn't going to work, Brad."

"Say what you really mean, Sarah."

The underlying steel in the soft command did nothing to alleviate the tension coiling inside her.

"Us. It's not going to work with us." Once started, the words tumbled out, burning her throat as they went. "I think I've known it all along, but I let myself believe it would all work out. I let you convince me that my— that things that matter very much don't matter at all."

The fatigue lines at the corners deepened as his eyes narrowed in confusion. "I'm missing something here, and it must be something very important, because I don't know what the hell you're getting at."

"I'm trying to tell you it's over, Brad."

"Why?" The word was a small explosion in the quiet room. "What happened between that loving welcome home on Friday and now to bring you to this absurd conclusion?"

"Everything that happened between Friday and now, that's what!" she cried, her stomach twisting into a knot. "It was obvious out there this weekend that I'm not at all suited to the things that are important to you."

Anger and disbelief mingled in the eyes boring into her. "You mean camping?"

"That's one thing, yes." She nodded her head vigorously. "You love it. I hate it."

"And because of that you're telling me to take a hike?"

"It's not just that." She closed her eyes and didn't open them until she was looking away from him. "It's the kids. You're so..."

"I thought we'd settled that. I've already told you I don't care that you're not able to have children."

"Well, I care," Sarah bit out. "And it's more than not being able to have them. I don't know if I even want them, if I would ever even want to adopt them."

He moved deliberately into her line of vision, impatience bracketing the hard slash of his mouth. "I wasn't planning on having that written into the marriage contract as a condition."

"We never said anything about marriage." Her words were as soft as his were loud.

"Didn't we?" he asked mockingly. "Well, I'm saying something about it now."

She closed her eyes, not wanting to watch her world crumbling around her. "Save your breath. There isn't going to be any marriage."

"Because you have some crazy idea that I want children more than I want you?"

"Because I know you will in the future." She was on her feet, trying to escape the anguished confusion in his eyes. "And because you should have children, Brad. You're a natural father. And I'd be no kind of mother at all."

He followed her to the window. His warm hands touched her shoulders gently. "How can you think that?"

"How can you not?" she cried, twisting from the false security of his hold. "You saw me this weekend. Face it, Brad, I could never be half the mother Nancy is."

"Nancy's had years of practice."

"It's more than practice; it's instinct. I just don't have it, and I don't have to adopt some poor, defenseless baby to prove that conclusively."

She moved again, putting the bentwood rocker between them, its curved wicker shape a flimsy barrier against the rage she sensed seething beneath his calmness.

"We're both very tired tonight, Brad. I really think it would be better for both of us if you left now." Then, her tone flat, drained of everything but the thread of self-control she was grasping like a lifeline, she quietly added, "I won't let you change my mind."

He watched her for a long time as she stood awkwardly, silently. His face was a tight, inscrutable mask. Finally he moved, walking slowly away from the door until he was close enough to touch her if he'd wanted to.

He spoke only one word. "No."

Sarah stared at him in confusion, trying to remember if she had asked a question.

"No, I won't leave," he clarified. "Not until we settle this to my satisfaction. If you think you can walk into my life and turn me inside out, then casually decide you don't feel like playing anymore, you're even stupider than you're acting tonight."

There was a gelid casing to each grim word. His eyes were like the night sky—deep, mysterious—and staring into them Sarah became belatedly aware that she was witnessing the dark side of a man's anger for the first time in her life. The side that bordered on desperation.

"What do you have to drink around here besides that godawful tea?" he asked roughly.

"There's some brandy in the kitchen cupboard."

When she didn't move to get it, he did, returning with two full glasses and the bottle tucked under one arm.

Sarah watched in silence while he drained his glass and splashed it full again.

Throwing himself down on the chintz-covered easy chair, he snarled, "I don't know how they can dignify this apricot stuff by calling it brandy."

"No one's twisting your arm to drink it," she returned, uneasy with this unexplored side of him.

He laughed, a bitter sound. "No, Sarah. It's not my arm your twisting, is it?"

"I resent that." She slammed her untouched glass down on the table.

"Not half as much as I resent your jerking me around this way."

"I'm not doing that." Her fingernails bit deeply into the soft flesh of her palms as she watched his dark eyebrows lift sardonically. "At least I don't want to do that. I asked you to leave just so we could avoid a scene like this. It's pointless."

"I'd say this little scene has a very definite point." His voice was firm, even, totally at odds with the fingers clenching his glass. "How else can I learn why you've been leading me on for weeks now? Was it just to keep me happy so I'd go along with your damn article, Sarah? I think I have a right to know."

She fought the pain his implication set coursing through her and seized the resentment that sizzled in its wake. "And I have a right to plan my own future, including deciding who will and won't be included in it."

"What about my rights?" he demanded, "What about the future I thought we could have together, the future *you* let me believe we could have?"

"It won't work." The cracking of her voice revealed more than was safe.

"You mean you won't even try."

Contempt threaded through his angry accusation, piercing something soft and fragile inside her, and Sarah knew if she didn't fight she would break. "You're damn right I won't try, not when the odds are stacked against me. I did that once, no, twice. And I'll never leave myself open to that kind of failure again."

"So now you're above failing?" he taunted, leaning into a pantherlike crouch at the cushion's edge.

"No, I'm not above it," she snapped, "but I don't go looking for it either."

"No, you'd rather go on living your safe little mediocre life than take a chance on real happiness."

"My life is not mediocre." Eyes flashing, she stepped closer to him. "This may come as a big surprise to you Mr. Success-and-Money, but I was not sitting around pining away before I met you."

"You're right. I'd say sitting around shriveling away is probably closer to the truth."

"How dare you say that to me?"

"You're going to find out I'll dare a hell of a lot more before I'll give you up."

"Why bother?" She tried and failed to keep the tears from her voice. "What would someone like you want with a shriveled up nobody like me?"

He swore softly and with one sleek stride was at her side, his powerful arms circling her despite her attempts to shove him away.

"Lord, I'm sorry, Sarah. I don't know what made me say any of that." His lips tousled her hair with small, frantic kisses. "You're far from being a nobody, and so far from being shriveled up it takes my breath away just to look at you."

His fury had been easy on her compared to this tender assault. Sarah knew that letting him touch her would be fatal to her resolve, so she frosted the air between them with a brittle, "Please let go of me."

Brad reluctantly lowered his arms, but his eyes caught hers and held them, reflecting a fire Sarah feared she was too drained to fight.

"I won't let you do this," he said softly.

"Then it's lucky for me I don't need your permission."

"Maybe not," His voice was low and as self-confident as his stance. "But you do need my cooperation. And there's no way I'll agree to stay away from you simply because you measured yourself against Nancy and think you came up short."

"Don't you understand it's because I refuse to measure myself against Nancy or anyone else that I'm doing this?" She shivered from the inside out, overwhelmed by the enormity of what she'd set in motion. "I tried to measure up to my parents' expectations and only ended up disappointing them and wasting years of my own life. And I tried to live up to what Rod expected and failed again— miserably. He didn't just drop me like a hot coal; he told me exactly and precisely how I had failed, how cold and unresponsive I was, even after I'd ignored my own instincts to become the kind of woman I thought he wanted."

Talking about it brought the pain back in slow-moving waves. Pain so intense it burned the tears away, and for the first time Sarah was grateful for the memory of that pain. It was all she had to pull her through this.

"But I promised myself a long time ago that would never happen to me again," she continued, her body taut as she strained for composure. "I control my life now. I know my limitations, and I accept them. I know my strengths as well. I have a job that I love and know I excel at."

"And that's enough?" he challenged.

"It has to be until I find something else I can do as well."

He stared at her incredulously for a minute. Then, very quietly, he said, "You're afraid."

That he had struck on the truth only made it worse. "Yes, I'm afraid. I'm afraid you'll lull me into thinking I can do something I can't, afraid of failing, afraid of being a disappointment to you. That would hurt more than I could stand," she finished, the raw state of her emotions painfully evident in every word.

"Come over here, Sarah, and let me show you how wrong that bastard was, how warm and responsive a woman you really are." His eyes smoldered over every inch of her, leaving no doubt about how he planned to prove his claim.

Sarah shook her head and backed another step away from him. "That wouldn't prove a thing. There's a lot more to being a woman than having sex, Brad."

"And more to it than having babies," he added, his eyes fastening on hers with a warmth that threatened to undermine her self-control in seconds flat. "Maternal instinct is not genetically linked to your reproductive organs, Sarah. It's a combination of desire and experience and a whole lot of trial and error. You think you'd be a washout if you had to step in and take over for Nancy tomorrow?" He waited for her to nod. "Well, do you think she'd fare any better if she had to take over your job on a moment's notice?"

"It's not the same thing," insisted Sarah, her chin lifting stubbornly.

"It's exactly the same thing. But Nancy's intelligent, and resourceful. She'd buckle under and somehow learn how to handle it. And so could you, if you'd stop feeling sorry for yourself long enough to take a chance on the future."

The blunt assessment stung. "I'm not feeling—"

"Yes, you are, and maybe you had good reason to back when this all happened. But you have to stop letting what you can't do blind you to all that you can. I'm not saying you're wrong not to want kids, but don't decide it by default. You have all the qualities any man could want in the mother of his children: understanding, compassion, a sense of humor."

He slid his fingers through her hair, rubbing her cheeks with hard palms. Sarah never realized a caress could feel hungry and gentle at the same time. His gaze moved over her face slowly, as if memorizing each detail of it was the most important thing in the world to him.

"It would work with us, Sarah." His voice was husky with the same yearning she read in his eyes. "It would work all the way. But I can't prove that to you in black and white. You seem to want some sort of up-front guarantee that you'll succeed before you'll even take the first step, and that's something all my money can't buy. I love you, Sarah. Tell me you don't need a guarantee. Tell me my love is enough."

His skilled touch and his soft words slipped the earth out from under her feet. She was suspended in air, the thrill and danger of it pulling her in opposite directions. Everything in her past had taught her to fight the feeling, taught her that keeping both feet planted firmly on the ground and avoiding the risk of the unknown were the cornerstones of survival.

"Tell me," he urged.

"I want to," she whispered, pressing her cheek against his hand once more before pulling away. "But I can't."

"No, Sarah, you choose not to. You're afraid to do the very thing you've been urging me to do all along: take a chance on the unknown. What's that old saying? Do as I—"

"Say, not as I do," Sarah finished, dropping her gaze to a suddenly fascinating piece of lint lying on the carpet between their feet.

He nodded. "That's the one. But I suppose I can't judge you too harshly. After all, I spent years thinking about whether the risk was worth taking, and then I had the luxury of thirty additional days just to make up my mind. But I'm not patient enough to wait years, Sarah. I can't even promise I'll be patient enough to leave you alone for thirty whole days, but we're going to give it a try."

"No."

"That wasn't a multiple-choice question. Actually it

wasn't a question at all. Thirty days."

Sarah drew a deep breath, unbelievably shaken by the impending desolation of thirty days without him. How would she ever reconcile herself to a lifetime of it?

"And if I still feel the same way then?"

A profound seriousness shadowed Brad's green eyes. He reached out and touched her face with one fingertip, a whisper of a caress that made her tremble. "Then we both lose."

She didn't watch him leave. She didn't even move for a long time after the door closed quietly behind him. When she did, it was a surprise to find that darkness had filled the room even as the color was slowly seeping from her life. She thought wearily that a rush of adrenaline wasn't the body's only method of dealing with a crisis. From some untapped chamber inside she was filled with a spreading numbness. She moved about the house on automatic pilot, unpacking her bag, taking a shower, getting her clothes ready for work in the morning just as if the sun would rise as usual. And when she fell into bed and a deep, undisturbed sleep hours later, she still hadn't cried.

She awoke with the same blessed feeling of numbness and the frightening realization that it couldn't last indefinitely. Fleeting images of breaking down in the middle of an editorial meeting or on the phone discussing business skittered through her mind as she drove to work. If Miriam or Melanie or anyone else noticed the robotlike way she moved through the day, they had the good grace not to mention it. Even when a small bunch of tiny blue flowers was delivered while she was spending her lunch hour running errands anyone else could have handled, Melanie simply placed them in a small vase on her desk without comment. There was no card, but Sarah didn't need one to tell her they were from Brad. They were forget-me-nots.

After the flowers, nothing. Great, yawning days full of it, days that ran together in her mind the way they tend to do when you're not sleeping nights. Predictably, the numbness wore off at bedtime on Monday night, leaving a deep, aching emptiness in its stead. Aching in more ways than she'd dreamed possible, in ways that radiated from deep inside her and spilled over into physical sensation, Sarah desperately clawed out a new and exhausting routine. She went to work each day, going through the motions of being a well-adjusted, functioning human being while life rolled on around her. She smiled and made decisions and feigned interest in the preparations for Saturday evening's banquet. Without warning the world sometimes blurred before her, running in smeared watercolors that she had to retreat to her office to bring under control.

At night she cleaned the house. All of it, from top to bottom, discovering nooks and crevices she never knew existed. The scrubbing and polishing had a distracting, tranquilizing effect that was infinitely better for her sanity than the utter desolation of lying in bed with only the all-night radio talk show for company. The idea that she might be trying to scrub every last trace of Brad from her world lurked somewhere on the fringes of Sarah's consciousness. Like anything related to Brad, she refused to let herself examine it too closely or for too long.

Day and night she suffered from chills that came out of nowhere and crept over her slowly, leaving everything a little more frozen, a little bleaker.

On Saturday she woke to a spit-shined house, a sunny day that threatened to be ages long, and the looming spectre of the banquet at the end of it. Without work as a reason to get out of bed, it suddenly became too much effort to do so. She lay tangled in the sheet, wearing a faded navy-blue T-shirt of Brad's that had somehow gotten mixed in with her things on the camping trip and that she had perversely been sleeping in ever since, and thought about the banquet.

She remembered the night of the party, when Brad had told her he would attend the banquet, for her, because of how much he loved her. She thought of how deep that love must run to prompt a man like Brad to do something that went against his grain, something he would find very uncomfortable, if not downright embarrassing, just because he thought it would please her. The memory loosed a flood of emotion that seeped from behind her stinging eyelids to soak the blue flowered pillow she was clutching.

The telephone's shrill, insistent ring cut short what promised to be a marathon crying jag. Wiping at her eyes with the corner of the sheet, Sarah rolled over and grabbed it on the ninth ring. She breathed a hoarse "Hello" into the receiver between alternate spurts of hope and dread that it might be Brad calling.

"Well, at long last."

The voice was feminine and patently disgusted, and Sarah's heart sank like a balloon full of lead.

"Oh, Julie. How are you?"

"What do you care? If you had a secretary at home to give me the brush-off, you wouldn't even be talking to me now."

"That's not true. I haven't been brushing you off." Sarah instantly cringed at the insulting half-truth and cut Julie's indignant retort short. "All right, I have been sort of avoiding your calls. But, Jul, I had good reason. I guess you know about Brad and me." Julie heard everything about everybody in town, and what she didn't know she was great at guessing.

"Yes, I know," she answered, all traces of resentment gone from her voice. "That's the reason I've been calling and the only reason I haven't shown up on your doorstep long before now. I figured you needed some time to sort things through on your own."

"Yeah, I guess that's what I've been doing." Sarah had to bite back a bitter laugh. Far from sorting her life back into anything resembling order, she felt as though she'd spent the last week falling from the bottom to some place much, much lower.

"Good, because I've given you all the time for that crap that I plan to. I want to have lunch. Today."

"Lunch?" The word came out haltingly, making Sarah sound vaguely confused.

"Right, lunch." Julie sighed. "You remember, that meal that comes smack in between breakfast and dinner."

Sarah remembered. She just couldn't remember eating any of those meals in the last five days, only an occasional half carton of yogurt or whatever else was already in the house and didn't dirty dishes or have to be cooked.

"I don't know, Julie. I have to get ready for tonight and—"

"Sarah," Julie interrupted in a tone that was exaggeratedly condescending, "try and remember who you're talking to—old never-take-no-for-an-answer Hazard. Now, do you want to haggle over this indefinitely, or are you going to shut up and agree to meet me at the Pirate's Den at one o'clock?"

"Sarah?" she repeated when the question was met with only silence. Then, louder, "Sarah, answer me."

"Well, which is it?" Sarah grumbled. "Shut up or answer you? I can't do both."

"Cute," Julie groaned, "very cute. It's such a relief to hear you haven't lost your sick sense of humor at least. I'll see you at one."

No, at least I haven't lost my sense of humor, Sarah thought bitterly as she hung up. It seemed meager consolation for all that she had lost, the scope and importance of which became more discouragingly obvious with each passing day. Brad's absence left a void that penetrated every level of her existence, a gaping chasm that seemed too enormous for any one man to fill. But Sarah knew without a doubt that one man, and one man only, could fill it, could make her whole again.

The Pirate's Den was a small waterside cafe not listed on any of Newport's tourist maps. Inside, there were a few booths with dark leather cushions and a large horseshoe bar, all of it dimly lit enough to keep the details of the decor a hazy secret, a fact Sarah suspected was a blessing for the patrons' appetites. She didn't share Julie's unbounded enthusiasm for the place, although she had to admit the food was probably a lot better than the intentions of a large part of the male clientele.

Julie was waiting when Sarah arrived, seated in a corner booth, ogling and being ogled by the motley crew at the bar. Sarah felt their collective attention shift to her as she passed by, and she held her breath until she was seated across from Julie.

"If I'd been more awake when you called this morning, I never would have agreed to meet you here," she said by way of greeting. "This place *looks* like a den for pirates."

"Why do you think I come here?" Julie shot back. "I keep hoping I'll pick one up."

"I'm more concerned about what I might pick up from the drinking glasses."

Grinning, Julie held her glass aloft. "Then order a whiskey neat. That'll burn the germs away before they can take hold."

"You'll understand if I'm not reassured by your grassroots scientific theory," Sarah replied.

"Probably not. I don't seem to understand as much about you as I thought I did." Julie's small smile disappeared as she studied Sarah's face critically. "You look like death warmed over."

Sarah straightened, self-consciously smoothing her hand over her hair. "I haven't been getting much sleep."

"Tell me something I can't see for myself," Julie snorted.

Before Sarah could respond, the waitress ambled over to take their order. Sarah pretended to read the menu, then listlessly echoed Julie's request for the lobster salad plate, substituting a glass of wine for the whiskey. She expected her friend to start in the moment they were alone, and when she didn't, Sarah began to suspect she was the victim of an approach more novel and well thought out than Julie's usual straightforward haranguing.

To test the theory, she casually asked what was new at the radio station, then went on to chat aimlessly about mutual friends, the crush of tourists, the weather. By the time two plates mounded with lobster chunks and crisp vegetable slices were placed in front of them, the topic of the day still remained untouched, and Sarah thought that if Julie's strategy was intended to set her on edge, it had certainly succeeded.

They both picked at their lunch until Sarah couldn't stand it another second. Pushing her plate away, she frowned across the table at Julie. "Listen, I know why you asked me to have lunch with you today, so why don't we just get it out into the open right now."

Julie's eyes widened with a degree of innocence Sarah knew she didn't possess. "Get what out in the open?"

"I hate it when you do that," Sarah hissed. "You know very well you brought me here to talk about—" The name stuck in her throat like a sharp-edged bone. "Brad. So go ahead and talk."

"You think I brought you here to pump you about what happened between you and Brad?"

"Didn't you?"

"No," Julie answered bluntly. "I know exactly what happened. Things got a little hot, Brad probably pressed for a commitment, and you backed off as if he were offering you a seat in the electric chair. And you can stop looking so betrayed; I did happen to run into Brad, but, gentleman that he is, he would only say that you've decided not to see each other for a while."

"That's what he thinks we're doing," Sarah said glumly.

"And what do you think?"

"I think I should never have listened to you in the first place." Anger without focus colored her words. "You're my best friend, Jul, but you're not me. I should have followed my own instincts from the start, the way I'm doing now. So you can just skip the lecture."

"No lecture," Julie promised. "Can we at least talk about it?"

"It won't help."

"It might help me. I feel responsible for bringing you and Brad together. You were right that first day; I did use your concern over the article as an excuse to get you to go out with him, and vice versa."

Sarah's sigh was heavy, tinged with pain. "You're not responsible. I knew what I was getting into from the start, and I just went ahead anyway."

"Was that so wrong?" Julie asked quietly.

"You see where it led."

"I see two people who are miserable, and I don't think either one knows why. I know Brad doesn't."

"I explained to him why it has to be this way."

"Then explain it to me."

"No." Sarah knew to attempt that would be to travel through the haphazard, bewildering world of Julie's reasoning. She wasn't up to the trip.

"Then let me explain it to you, in your own terms." She silenced Sarah's protest with a stubborn look Sarah knew better than to argue with. "I know your reason for breaking it off with Brad has to have something to do with the fact that you can't have children. I'm sure in your mind the connection between the two is very clear cut, so I've spent all week trying to understand why."

Sarah tossed down the napkin she'd been twisting

between her fingers. "Look, Julie, I appreciate your concern—"

"Then show it by listening to what I have to say," Julie interrupted firmly. "I started out by asking myself, 'How would Sarah approach this whole thing?' and I think you're going to be real proud of what I came up with." Smiling smugly, she leaned forward and rested her chin on her laced fingers. "Logic."

"I'd say astounded is closer to what I feel," Sarah replied.

Julie ignored the not-so-subtle slur. "I remembered how impressed you were by all those principles and propositions of logical thought when you studied it back in college, so it was a sure bet you'd use a few to handle a dilemma this size."

"So you decided to do the same?" A small smile, her first of the week, teased Sarah's lips as the diametrically opposed notions of Julie's reasoning and the discipline of logic collided in her mind.

Julie nodded. "And didn't do a half-bad job of it, if I do say so myself."

"You must have had to start by looking up the definition of *logic* in the dictionary."

"Of course," Julie admitted unabashedly. "All that deductive reasoning mumbo jumbo isn't the sort of thing I like to have cluttering up my mind on a regular basis. Now, would you like to hear what I've deduced?"

"Do I have a choice?" Sarah asked, lifting her hands in surrender.

"Not if you want to get rid of me in time for tonight's banquet," retorted Julie, settling herself for what was obviously going to be a siege. "According to the dictionary, logic is simply the relationship of element to element in a whole in a set of objects, individuals, principles, or events."

She responded with an indignant frown when Sarah broke into quiet applause at the end of the recitation, then continued. "Obviously, what we're dealing with here are events. Namely, the eventual outcomes of the two possible courses of action open to you concerning your future with Brad."

Sarah could feel herself tensing up as the discussion narrowed from the general to the very personal. She knew Julie, and she knew this exaggeratedly detailed attempt at logic was in all likelihood a carefully camouflaged steel trap.

"And what two courses of action are those?" she asked carefully.

"Why, continuing the relationship or ending it, of course," Julie replied. "Being a diehard romantic, I naturally considered the possibility of continuing it first, and I'm glad I did. I think I can see exactly where the problem lies in that approach. The great unknown."

"The great unknown?" Sarah repeated, hearing the steel trap slowly cranking shut with her inside.

"Right—the future. We can't see it, so it falls into that class of elements not based on observable data. Of course there is the possibility it could turn out to be pure bliss for the two of you, which would make any risk involved well worth taking. But we can't ignore the other possibility, can we? That for personal reasons, which are extremely valid, it might not work out. Then you'd be left without the storybook ending, without Brad, and without even the relatively happy life you had before he came along. I mean good friends and a job you enjoy would hardly be compensation for all you stand to lose."

"Hardly," agreed Sarah, her tone stiff and remote. Julie's approach to logical reasoning was leaving a sour feeling of apprehension in the pit of her stomach.

"So if this logic stuff is all it's cracked up to be," Julie went on with a look of thoughtful bewilderment Sarah wasn't buying for a second, "why does the flip side of this situation bother me so much?"

Sarah didn't even attempt to reply. She sensed that

Julie had the answer ready and had been craftily leading Sarah up to it since the moment she walked into the place.

Julie didn't smile as she leaned forward. "I mean if you do opt for the second course of action, as logic seems to dictate, and give Brad the gate, as you so wisely have decided to do"—there was a blatant challenge in every word and in the blue eyes that held Sarah's relentlessly—"exactly what do you have left that's worth all you've paid?"

Chapter Ten

THE ANSWER, OF COURSE, was as obvious as Julie's little performance.

Nothing Sarah had ever had in the past or could hope to attain in the future would ever equal the splendor of Brad's love. Staring at each other across the table in the smoke-filled Pirate's Den, both women knew it. After a long enough pause to make her point, Julie graciously let Sarah off the hook with a casual, "Think it over."

Sarah didn't stop thinking about it all the way home. Then she turned the car's engine off and sat in front of the house and thought about it some more. No matter how she tried to fight the truth or temper it with old fears and doubts, one facet shone through like a diamond in sunlight: Sharing her future with Brad wouldn't be *taking* a chance on happiness. It was her *only* chance. Without him, the pleasant delusion her life had once been would seem an unbearable sham.

With that relization came the certain knowledge of what she had to do, and driving through the busy streets between her house and Brad's, Sarah felt lighter and freer and happier than she had ever thought to feel again. Even the locked gates and silent intercom that greeted her couldn't dull her mood. But at seven o'clock that evening, after another trip out to Brad's and countless attempts to reach him by telephone, she was beginning to feel frantic around the edges.

What she wanted to do was sit there and let his phone ring until he returned home to pick it up. What she had to do was get dressed and drag herself down to the Marble House, where the cocktail reception preceding the banquet was about to begin. Sarah knew Miriam was counting on her to be there, and, above and beyond the call of duty, she liked her boss too much to let her down. Even if it meant endless hours of smiling and laughing and being courteous to advertisers and dancing with men whose touch would make her skin crawl after it had known the magic of being touched by a man with haunting green eyes.

Sarah showered quickly and slipped into the ivory silk dress overlaid with lace she'd bought in anticipation of sharing this evening with Brad. The pounds she'd lost the hard way over the past few days heightened the effect of the tightly sashed waist, and if the creamy color did the same for her paleness, she just had to hope the lighting at the Marble House would be soft enough to conceal the fact. With her hair piled loosely on top of her head and a single strand of pearls enhancing the scalloped neckline, she decided she looked as close to gorgeous as she could hope to without Brad by her side.

She knew the secret of the dress's impact lay in its demureness, in the clever way it hinted at the sensuality of the woman inside, and she longed to see the aura of romance it cast reflected in Brad's eyes. There was little chance of that. Intoxicating as she found the thought of his missing her so much he'd break his vow to stay away for thirty days, she doubted he would ever choose a place as public as the banquet to do it.

At the last minute she decided to call a cab for the short drive to Bellevue Avenue, simply to avoid the embarrassment of pulling up to the Marble House unescorted in a car that threatened to die a noisy death at any moment. The renowned mansion was already ablaze with activity when she arrived, sparkling with the sights and sounds of a gala event Sarah felt must rival the lavish parties of the days when the wealthy Vanderbilt family called this home.

In the grand ballroom, resplendent in sumptuous hues of scarlet and ornate gilt trim, tuxedoed gentlemen and ladies in long, flowing gowns strolled about sipping champagne. At one end of the long room stretched an elaborately arranged head table; at the other, an orchestra played a waltz for the couples gliding across the mirrorlike dance floor. Despite her initial opposition to the whole affair, Sarah had to admit the arrangements had been handled with excellent taste and more than a dash of elegance. However, that didn't make being stuck there any less distressing.

The feeling started as a small seed of desperation that grew and flourished as she did the mingling she knew was expected of her. It tied her stomach in knots and made it extremely difficult to pretend she was thrilled to meet the gynecologist who had edged Brad out of the running and suffer through a dance full of his cute little professional jokes. The second it was over she dumped him on poor Melanie and went out of her way to avoid another introduction at Miriam's hands. And all the time she was smiling, nodding, and moving from group to group of people whose names she forgot as soon as she heard them, she was wondering where Brad would be.

He'd once joked about the stigma of being dateless on a Saturday night, and for an instant Sarah worried that he might be free of that stigma tonight. She forced the thought from her mind. Julie had said that Brad looked as miserable as she did, and everything she knew about him told her he was not the sort of man who'd try to drown his sorrow in another woman. Now, a bottle of Jack Daniels—that was another matter altogether. Immediately Sarah thought of the small waterfront bar his sailing cronies called their own.

Knowing full well that staying at least until after dinner was the responsible, professional thing to do, she started walking toward the elaborately carved archway that formed the ballroom's entrance. Her steps quickened as she moved along the wide hallway illuminated by massive crystal chandeliers, and by the time she reached the gracefully curving marble staircase she was almost running. The stairs were wide and highly polished, and Sarah had her eyes focused cautiously on her feet as she hopped from the bottom step and plowed straight into a wall of steel wearing a black tuxedo.

Before she had a chance to recover, strong arms reached out, steadying her and keeping her close at the same time, and a deep voice asked, "How do you feel about dancing with a loser, sweet lady?"

Her eyes flew up past the crisp white shirt and black bow tie to meet green ones brimming with love. Joy started as a whisper deep inside her. "Oh, Brad, you're not drunk."

"No," he agreed, breaking into a grin that bared teeth and dimples, "but I will be if you keep looking at me that way."

Sarah sighed and rubbed her cheek against his chest, heedless of the latecomers stepping around them to climb the stairs. "Then you'll have to stay drunk, because I plan to keep looking at you this way for a long, long time."

The words struck home. Sarah could feel the questioning tension in Brad recede as he gazed at her with much the same look she was giving him.

"I think I can learn to take it." He held her face

between his palms and lightly stroked the fragile skin beneath her eyes. "You look beautiful, Sarah, even with dark circles under your eyes. Lord, I've missed you."

Like an arid sponge, Sarah absorbed the adoration in his tone. It was heaven to feel again the sweet, flooding pleasure loosed by his touch.

"I've been calling you all day," she said dreamily, "and I drove out to your house, twice."

"I was at the shipyard," he explained. "I've been going out at sunrise every day, trying to lose myself in work."

"I was afraid you were trying to lose yourself in a bottle."

"I tried a little of that, too," Brad admitted sheepishly, "but around about Wednesday I made a discovery of unprecedented importance: I can't work enough or drink enough to keep you off my mind."

His fingers moved slowly over her lace-covered shoulders, brushing her senses to tingling awareness.

"I think our weeks had a lot in common," breathed Sarah.

"I discovered something else this week." He tipped her face up to his. "Without you in my life, what's left isn't worth a damn."

"Brad, have you by any chance been talking to Julie?" Laughter hovered just beneath her words.

He nodded, grinning. "Just a little while ago. I never realized she was so well schooled in logic."

"I'm not sure she is." Her laughter evaporated as she searched Brad's eyes. "I'm not sure there's anything logical about this at all."

"Then God save us from logic," he declared, "because this is what I want. I wanted to give you time—time to think, time to miss me a little—but I couldn't. Even before Julie came out to the house I'd decided I was coming here to find you tonight. I can't give you distance, Sarah. And I can't give you up."

She felt the warm security of his love flow through her. "I don't want you to give me time or distance ever again."

"What do you want, Sarah? Why were you trying to reach me?" A look of hope gleamed like silver in his eyes, commanding the words from her.

Sarah smiled up at him, feeling through the smooth black fabric of his jacket the pounding of a heart strong enough to build a future on. Any last, lingering traces of doubt fell away. "To tell you that this is what I want, too; that loving you is worth any risk, any sacrifice."

She watched relief and desire play over his face, casting velvet shadows over its chiseled lines. The knowledge of where they were kept them from touching except for their tightly clasped hands, but something elemental in Sarah reached out to him and was not disappointed. She felt the fire and love in him as surely as she felt her heart beating, and love washed over her in a dizzying torrent.

When Brad spoke again, his voice was husky, deceptively composed. "As long as that's settled, shall we go upstairs to the banquet?"

His mention of the banquet hit her like a bucket of icy water, and even as he hooked her arm through his, guilt, embarrassment, and concern merged to tint her cheeks crimson.

"Oh, no!" she exclaimed, swinging around to block his path. "We can't go up there, not until I tell you . . . You see, things have been so crazy the past few weeks, first with you going away and all, that I never quite told you . . ."

"That I'd been canned from the article," he finished for her, his eyes filled with loving amusement.

Sarah chewed nervously on her bottom lip. "How did you know?"

"Relax, love. Nancy let it slip while we were camping.

I figured you'd get around to telling me sooner or later in your own roundabout way."

"I didn't want to tell you on the phone," she explained hurriedly, "I was afraid you might be disappointed, especially after you'd mentioned it to some of your friends. Then, whenever we were together, I got sidetracked."

His fingers teased the softness at the inside of her elbow, then followed a trail of goosebumps up to her shoulder. "I can see how that could easily happen. Before it happens here, in front of those two very interested doormen, maybe we should go upstairs and have that dance. At least I'll have a legitimite excuse to put my arms around you."

Sarah stayed right where she was, shaking her head slowly.

"You don't want to dance?" asked Brad.

"I don't want to dance here," she explained, lowering her eyes as surprised awareness flickered in his.

"I see." A mischievous smile creased his mouth. "But if we leave now, we'll miss the best part of the evening."

Her eyes, when she lifted them again, glittered with laughter, and her sultry smile was a match for his any day.

"I don't think so, Brad. I really don't think so."

They left quickly, but the ride along Ocean Drive to his house seemed unbearably long, and Sarah found herself wishing the road, with its picturesque twists and dips along the rocky coastline, was as straight as the crow flies. Brad had ignored the pointed suggestion that her place was closer, and now she had to content herself with the slow trickle of his fingers over her leg and an occasional long, steamy glance that set her senses hammering with an exhilaration that grew and grew until she felt as if she were drowning in it.

The feeling seemed to reach a crescendo when they passed through the gates onto his property, but instead of veering off the drive at the cottage, Brad followed its graceful curl to the front of the main house. Silencing the engine, he faced Sarah's questioning glance with a rather serious expression.

"I'd like to show you the house, if you're interested," he began hesitantly. "It occurred to me as I lay awake in bed night after night this past week how many things we've never done together. We've never seen snow together, or a thunderstorm. We've never made love outside on the beach." He reached for her hand and carried it to his lips. "I never showed you the place where I grew up, even though you once asked to see it."

"You seemed put off by the idea," Sarah said quietly. "I didn't want to press."

"Press, please," he implored. "Sometimes that's exactly what I need." He propped his arms on the steering wheel and peered through the front window, a strange, contemplative expression in his eyes as they roamed over the stately brick structure before them. "I have such mixed feelings about this place. I couldn't wait to move out when it was time to go away to school, and I don't think you could say I ever actually missed it." A rueful smile tugged at his mouth. "And yet when my parents wanted to turn it over to the Historical Society as a tax write-off when they moved to Florida, I offered to buy it from them instead."

"And then promptly moved down to the guest house," added Sarah, reaching over to rub the tension from his neck muscles.

"Crazy, huh?" He laughed and arched his neck in appreciation of her tender ministrations. "I think in the back of my mind I planned some sort of revenge on the old place, as if by someday filling it with children and laughter I could wipe away the loneliness of my own childhood." His quick glance at Sarah was full of loving concern. "I didn't say that to hurt you."

"I know you didn't," she said quietly. Then, taking

a deep breath, she added, "Besides, I think it sounds like a great idea." It was meant as an offering, an expression of how deeply she trusted in their love, but Brad was shaking his head.

"I have a better one. I did a lot of thinking this week, about what I thought I wanted out of life, and about what I want now. I meant what I said a while ago: Without you, nothing else matters anymore. I could have kids hanging from the rafters of this place and still be lonely as hell if you weren't with me." His smile was warm and beseeching, and it made Sarah's breath catch. "On the other hand, I know you and I alone could fill it with enough happiness to chase away all my ghosts."

For a moment she was lost in the headiness of being loved by such a man. Then the full impact of what he'd said came tumbling over her, and her astonished eyes met his expectant green ones.

"You mean live here?"

"Why not?" he countered amiably. "There's certainly plenty of room, you can't beat the neighborhood, and I think the private beach out back will prove very handy come summer."

The sexiness of his throaty chuckle was momentarily wasted on Sarah. She hadn't had time to think beyond the wonder of their being back together to such symbols of permanency as where they might live. The sheer opulence of his suggestion floored her.

"I don't know, Brad."

"You will as soon as you get a look at the inside," he assured her, getting out of the car and sliding her along with him. "It has all the basics."

"Like running water, heat, electricity," she teased.

"Right. Along with six bedrooms, a library, solarium, music room, butler's pantry—"

"A butler's pantry," Sarah drawled with a careless wave of her arm. "I don't know how I've survived all these years without one."

"Well, now you won't have to." Opening the door, he reached inside for a switch that seemed to turn on lights in every room in the house. He took her hand firmly in his, and together they stepped into the spacious, marble-floored foyer. "I think I'll save carrying you over the threshold until I've earned the right."

A shiver danced along Sarah's spine at what the husky comment implied, and it took a moment for her to come back to earth enough to absorb the magnificence all around them. When she did, she turned back to him, awed.

"Brad, this is beautiful."

"Don't try to spare my feelings," he ordered, leading her into the living room. "I didn't do the decorating, and I know it's a bit ostentatious in places." He tugged at a red brocade drape. "And somewhat tacky in others." He stopped wandering to point at the portrait of a somber, rather bull-faced old gentleman in a a heavily scrolled gold frame. "Reginald somebody-or-other," he explained in answer to her unspoken question. "My great-uncle, I think."

Sarah reached up and cupped Brad's face in her hands, turning it this way and that in the light. "Yes, I can see the resemblance," she lied, fighting to hold back a bubble of laughter. "Especially around the mouth."

"Funny you should mention that." His eyes glittered a belated warning as his hands came up to cover hers, holding them against his skin. "You have to be very careful of the Chandler mouth. Its power is legendary."

With each husky word his head dipped lower, lower, until that legendary mouth touched hers with fire. His lips parted, moving hungrily, whispering words of desire that stirred something wild inside Sarah. With meticulous care he wet her lips, coasting from corner to corner and back until they glistened with the taste of him and Sarah ached for more. She savored the ache, deepening it by arching against him, secure in the knowledge that it would soon be lovingly assuaged.

When his gentle assault took him beyond her obligingly parted lips, she let her eyes close, turning the world into a chamber of darkness ruled by the tantalizing sweetness of his tongue dancing against hers. Her hands slid from beneath his, finding their way into the dark waves of his hair, while Brad's slipped lower, searching out the tender spot where her pulse fluttered in her throat. He circled it slowly with his thumb: then, with a groan of frustration, he shifted to rest his forehead against hers. The sound of his labored breathing mingled with the broken pattern of her own.

When he finally lifted his head, his eyes were dark with desire. "Come on. I suppose I should finish the tour, if only as a clever ruse to get you up to one of the bedrooms."

"Do you think you could be clever quickly?" she asked, her voice touched with wistfulness. "It's been such a long week."

Laughing softly, he kissed the top of her head, then kept his arm around her waist as they hurried through the rest of the first floor, his touch a constant, gentle tug on the streamers of desire he'd unfurled within her. Enchantment gradually overtook Sarah's feelings of trepidation as she discovered window seats, secret passages, and other touches of elegance from another century. Upon discovering the butler's pantry was simply a small serving and storage area between the kitchen and dining room, she feigned disappointment.

"It's just a plain old pantry," she complained. "I expected something a little grander."

"But at least it has a dumbwaiter," Brad offered, laughing and showing her. "That should count for something."

"You sound as if you're trying to sell me the place."

He leaned back against a wall of cupboards and pulled her against him. His face was suddenly very serious. "Actually, I'm trying to give it to you. But there is one slight hitch: I come along with it."

"A package deal?" Sarah strained for lightness as sky-rockets exploded inside. "I suppose that's for the best. After all, a dumbwaiter isn't much company."

Hopefulness made his eyes burn bright. "Does that mean you'll marry me?"

"It means if you don't hurry up and ask me outright, I'll be forced to ask you."

He smiled that lazy, crooked smile she adored. "I think I'd like that. It would sure be a big change from the woman who would never say what she really meant, or ask for what she really wanted."

"I'm asking now." She held his gaze, her eyes luminous with love. "I want you, Brad. Will you marry me?"

Instantly she was scooped up in his strong arms and twirled around and around in the small room. His actual reply, if there was one, was quite incoherent, but Sarah could tell from the jubilation in his laugh that it was an unqualified yes. She wrapped her arms around his neck and kissed the warm skin below his ear until his head lowered and his mouth moved across hers with a hunger magnified by the days of separation and sweetened by the promise of all the days and nights to come.

Still holding her, he strode back toward the stairs, mounting them with an urgency that flowed from him in bolts Sarah could feel.

"I take it this means the tour is over," she teased, tugging at the knot of his bow tie.

His soft laugh was frankly erotic, like the impulse it sent whipping through her. "Most definitely. I've decided I'd much rather spend the rest of the night exploring you."

The hand that had been riding her ribcage moved, inching higher as he climbed. When it found the soft curve of her breast the arms holding her quivered, but Sarah knew she was safe. She knew she'd always be safe with this man whose touch had taught her more about being a woman than she'd known there was to learn. There was only one small revelation still standing between her and utter happiness. As they reached the top of the stairs she touched his face hesitantly.

"Brad...about children..."

"Not now, Sarah," he groaned huskily, turning to capture her fingers with his mouth. His tongue licked their tips, sending a spasm of pleasure straight to her core.

"Yes, now," she insisted, pulling her fingers from the furnace of his mouth.

Brad stopped dead in his tracks with a deep sigh of resignation and stared down at her expectantly. The smoldering pleasure within made each thought, each word, a heroic effort, and Sarah searched for the right words to tell him of her decision, determined that there be no disharmony, no reservations lingering between them when they came to each other.

"I'm still not sure I'll make a good mother," she began haltingly, "but maybe I could sort of test the waters by spending more time with Tommy and the twins." She licked her lips, staring into the emerald depths of his eyes. "If you're willing to take a chance on me, then I'm willing, too."

"Thank you," he said, his voice deep, hushed. "It's more than I would ever ask."

Sarah knew that, and the fact that he would never ask made her all the more willing to give and give until the lines separating her from him blurred into obscurity.

He started down the hallway, dropping kisses on her smiling, upturned face. "The walk to my room never seemed so long before." Then, grimacing at the flocked gold wallpaper, he muttered, "Remind me to get rid of that along with the drapes and Uncle Reggie's picture."

Laughing, Sarah arched her neck so his lips could play along its smooth line, then twisted upright to look over his shoulder as a fleeting glimpse of something light and lacy caught her eye.

"Brad, stop. Can I peek in there?"

She pointed to the room they'd just passed, its mahogany door open wide, and he obligingly backed up. Soft yellow light spilled into the room from the hallway, adding to the ethereal mood. Aside from the rich tones of the cherrywood furniture, the only other color in the room was ivory. The plush carpet, satin coverlet, and lacy curtains were all variations of the same soft, creamy shade. Most alluring to Sarah was the canopy bed in the center of the room, the sheer lace curtains at each corner falling from a ruffled valance and held in loose gathers by satin ribbons.

"One of the guest rooms," Brad explained. Then, shaking his head in despair, he said, "Obviously not decorated during my mother's functionalist period. Add it to the list of things that have to go."

"Not on your life," breathed Sarah, spellbound by the room that suddenly seemed a perfect part of this heavenly night. "I love it. It's like a fantasy come to life."

A wry smile drifted across Brad's features. "Not one of *my* fantasies. If they feature any lace at all, it's usually black or red."

"Couldn't you make an exception, just this once?" she asked, touching his lips with her fingertips, her words a husky, feminine purr.

Brad seemed to forget the question as he licked at her fingers. Then, trying his best to frown, he groused, "I wanted to make love to you in my bed."

"They're all your beds," Sarah pointed out practically. She followed up on her statement by stringing tiny, frivolous kisses along his jaw, loving the age-old lovers' game and knowing he did, too.

She didn't even have to say "please." A tremor quaked through him as he stepped farther into the room and let her glide down his body until she was standing on the thick, pale carpet before him.

"Anything for the lady with the hungry blue eyes," he murmured, taking her lips in a kiss that set a torch to her blood.

"I love you, Brad," she whispered when he dipped to bring his kiss to her throat, licking a line down to the barrier of her dress. Desire rippled in her voice and started a warm, thrilling tensing in her belly.

Without breaking the contact between his lips and her flesh, he turned her slowly until her back was to him, then reached for her zipper. He lowered it with agonizing patience, warming each inch of exposed skin thoroughly with his mouth before moving lower. By the time he peeled the dress off her entirely, every nerve in Sarah's body was shimmering out of control, throbbing with need. Still he held to a snail's pace, sliding her out of her slip and underclothes, touching her all over with the softness and warmth of a summer breeze.

The soft glow from the hall outlined their shadows on the bedroom wall so Sarah could see the hazy echo of each caress, could watch in mounting fascination as he bathed her body with the magic of his touch. Finally, adrift on an ocean of sensation, she saw his hands lift to her shoulders and felt him turning her back to face him.

"Your turn, love," he prompted, his eyes glittering with arousal, his deep, raspy voice radiating sexual heat.

Delighted, Sarah slipped off his jacket and finished unknotting his tie, letting it hang open as she moved on to the studs securing the front of the pleated dress shirt, then eased that off, too.

"I've never undressed you completely," she whispered, touching his bare chest, loving the sound of him sucking in his breath.

"That's because I've never had the patience." His chuckle had a thrilling choppiness. "And I'm not sure I have it tonight."

"I'll hurry," Sarah said, but she didn't.

She treated him to the same lavishly detailed attention she had received, sliding his belt free of his pants, then dragging them to the floor, caressing each inch of rock-hard muscle along the way. She could feel the tremors of his mounting passion as she repeated the process with his shorts, then stepped back, fire in her eyes at the sight of his lean, bronze body.

"You're perfect," she breathed, letting him pull her close, feeling him begin to weave his magic the instant his fingers touched her.

He laughed and repeated the flick of his tongue that had made her purr and arch against him. "As perfect as a loser can be."

"A loser?" echoed Sarah, trying to latch on to the velvet wave of his words. "Oh, you mean the article." She shivered as his wandering mouth found the peak of her breast and tugged. "There's always next year. Tonight was such a success Miriam said it's going to become an annual event."

The earth tilted as she was swept up in his arms.

"That's good news." He smiled down at her from beneath a smoldering green gaze. "Do you think being married to the editor will give me a leg up on the competition?"

"I might be able to put in a good word for you," Sarah offered, wrapping her arms around his neck and teasing his chin with her tongue. "If you do *everything* I say."

He tumbled her onto the satin glow of the bedspread and stood hesitantly, feigning reluctance. "You mean for the whole next year?"

"Actually, I was thinking more like the next fifty or sixty."

A spark of a wicked smile, a flash of dimple, and then he lowered his body to cover hers.

"My sweet lady, you've got yourself a deal."

WONDERFUL ROMANCE NEWS:

Do you know about the exciting SECOND CHANCE AT LOVE/TO HAVE AND TO HOLD newsletter? Are you on our *free* mailing list? If reading all about your favorite authors, getting sneak previews of their latest releases, and being filled in on all the latest happenings and events in the romance world sounds good to you, then you'll love our SECOND CHANCE AT LOVE and TO HAVE AND TO HOLD Romance News.

If you'd like to be added to our mailing list, just fill out the coupon below and send it in...and we'll send you your *free* newsletter every three months — hot off the press.

☐ *Yes, I would like to receive your free SECOND CHANCE AT LOVE/TO HAVE AND TO HOLD newsletter.*

Name _____

Address _____

City _____ **State/Zip** _____

Please return this coupon to:

Berkley Publishing
200 Madison Avenue, New York, New York 10016
Att: Irene Majuk

HERE'S WHAT READERS ARE SAYING ABOUT

Second Chance at Love

"I think your books are great. I love to read them, as does my family."
— *P. C., Milford, MA**

"Your books are some of the best romances I've read."
— *M. B., Zeeland, MI**

"SECOND CHANCE AT LOVE is my favorite line of romance novels."
— *L. B., Springfield, VA**

"I think SECOND CHANCE AT LOVE books are terrific. I married my 'Second Chance' over 15 years ago. I truly believe love is lovelier the second time around!"
— *P. P., Houston, TX**

"I enjoy your books tremendously."
— *I. S., Bayonne, NJ**

"I love your books and read them all the time. Keep them coming—they're just great."
— *G. L., Brookfield, CT**

"SECOND CHANCE AT LOVE books are definitely the best.!"
— *D. P., Wabash, IN**

*Name and address available upon request

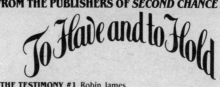